He couldn't believe where he was.

In his daughter's room. Putting her to bed.

"Don't go, Daddy."

He wanted to tell her he'd never leave her. That even though they'd just met, she was one of the most important people to him. Sadness threatened him as he thought of everything that running away, being a coward, had cost him.

"I'm here, baby girl."

Piper said her prayers and ended it with a line that clogged emotion in his th___. "And thank You for bringing Daddy hom___

Wade kissed her cheek. "___

He placed a hand on ___ guided her into the hallwa___ ___ to face him, tears rolled ___ ___ ugged her, but she stiffen___ ___ ducking into her own bed___

Seeing Cassidy c___ ___ being able to fix it felt like a knife to th___ ___st.

Tucking Piper in tonight had been one of the best moments of his life.

But now he had to leave. Because he was flirting with danger. The danger of falling for Piper's mother.

Avid reader, coffee drinker and chocolate aficionado **Jessica Keller** has degrees in communications and biblical studies and spends too much time on Instagram and Pinterest. Jessica calls the Midwest home. She lives for fall, farmers' markets and driving with the windows down. To learn more, visit Jessica at www.jessicakellerbooks.com.

Books by Jessica Keller

Love Inspired

Red Dog Ranch

The Rancher's Legacy
His Unexpected Return

Goose Harbor

The Widower's Second Chance
The Fireman's Secret
The Single Dad Next Door
Small-Town Girl
Apple Orchard Bride
The Single Mom's Second Chance

Lone Star Cowboy League: Boys Ranch

The Ranger's Texas Proposal

Home for Good

Visit the Author Profile page at Harlequin.com for more titles.

His Unexpected Return

Jessica Keller

HARLEQUIN® LOVE INSPIRED®

Recycling programs for this product may not exist in your area.

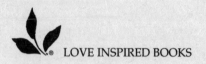

LOVE INSPIRED BOOKS

ISBN-13: 978-1-335-47945-7

His Unexpected Return

Copyright © 2019 by Jessica Koschnitzky

www.Harlequin.com

Printed in U.S.A.

And I will restore to you the years
that the locust hath eaten.
—*Joel* 2:25

For anyone who has ever wanted a second chance.

Chapter One

"Can I go swimming, Mommy?" Piper tugged on Cassidy Danvers's hand. At almost five, Piper had already perfected the art of the doe-eyed pout.

Cassidy pulled her apron over her head, then set it on the wall of hooks at the back of the kitchen. She turned and eyed the bright pink cast on Piper's arm. Even when Cassidy plastered every inch of her daughter's arm in obscene amounts of plastic wrap or used a long bread bag to cover it, Piper had a hard time keeping the cast from getting wet while taking a bath. With her enthusiasm and daring, going in the pool sounded disastrous. Cassidy's daughter had missed her best friend's pool-themed birthday party the prior weekend, so it wasn't the first time they were having the conversation, but if Piper was anything it was determined.

Piper noticed where her eyes fell. "I'll be so careful." She tucked her little casted arm behind her back as if keeping it from Cassidy's view would somehow make her mom forget about the injury. "You'll see. It will be fine. I just want to swim, Mom. One time."

"Baby girl." Cassidy dropped to her knees in the middle of the industrial kitchen where she spent most of her time. Despite the large window AC unit blasting wave after wave of cold air across her skin, the smell of burger grease lingered in the air from dinner. As head cook at the ranch, Cassidy was used to the smell—used to the four walls that made up the dining hall at Red Dog Ranch.

Her safe place.

After a tornado had torn its way through the ranch only weeks ago, the dining hall had been one of the first buildings the work crews had put back together. The owner, Rhett Jarrett, had insisted upon it. Outside, however, at least half of the ranch was still in shambles. Organized shambles, of course, but there was still so much to rebuild.

Too much.

After such destruction, Cassidy wondered if the ranch would ever truly be put back together again. In her life, that had never been the case. Trauma left scars.

Strands of hair had escaped the twin braids hanging over each of Piper's shoulders. Cassidy brushed the errant wisps away from her daughter's face, then let her hands cup Piper's rounded cheeks. Piper had Cassidy's brown eyes, but her daughter's hair and expressions were the same as her father's had been. *Wade.* Cassidy's heart squeezed at the thought of him like it always did. Even though his funeral had been five years ago, memories of him invaded her life every day.

"Only one more week left until the cast comes off." Cassidy let her hands fall to Piper's tiny shoulders, offering a light squeeze. "Let's hold off swimming until then. We can do that or something else fun to celebrate. It'll be your choice."

Piper huffed. "But it's so hot out. Even my knees are sweating."

Cassidy chuckled. "It's called summer in Texas, sweetheart. We've got hot days and hotter days. Take your pick."

"Uncle Rhett said if you said no to the pool, then I should ask about the sprinkler."

"Did he now?" Cassidy's voice warmed. Piper's uncle Rhett was the new owner of Red Dog Ranch. He had inherited the family estate two months ago and was now devoting every spare minute to rebuilding the ranch in time to host free summer programs for foster kids—a longtime mission of the ranch. But he always made time for Piper.

Piper nodded solemnly. "And Aunt Shannon told me she broke her arm one time when she fell from a tree. The same one that I broke. Isn't that neat?" Piper put up her good hand when Cassidy opened her mouth to respond. She was about to explain falling from trees was actually not neat at all. Cassidy loved that Piper was adventurous, but her daughter hardly needed encouragement or ideas that might get her hurt again.

Piper leaned closer, her excitement palpable. "That's not even the best part. Shannon said Grandma still let her swim in the pond and tube on the river with her cast. She just made her wear a bread bag with a rubber band over her arm. Just like I do for tubs!" Piper drew a line on her bicep, showing where the rubber band fit.

Cassidy tapped her chin, making a show of giving it all some thought. "Sounds like I need to tell Shannon and Rhett they're not allowed to gang up on me like this."

"No, Mommy." Piper's eyes widened. "I like playing with them. Don't—"

"I'm only kidding, sweetheart." Cassidy pulled her daughter in for a tight hug. She pressed a kiss to the top of her head. "Well, what are we waiting for? Sounds like it's time to go to the big house and see if the bag we used for last night's bath is still hole-free."

"Really?" Piper grinned like it was Christmas. "We can? You promise?"

"Of course. But only to jump through the sprinkler." Cassidy flipped off the lights in the kitchen and took Piper's hand, ushering her through the expansive dining area, where they weaved around all the tables to get to the front door at the other end of the building. Red Dog Ranch usually functioned as a summer camp for foster children. That was the reason why the dining hall had been built initially, but it was also where meals were served for the staff that lived on the property year-round.

Cassidy held the cumbersome front door of the dining hall open for Piper, then she followed her outside. Bright sunlight momentarily blinded her. She cast her eyes down. Positioned beside the small chapel on a hill that overlooked the ranch, the dining hall got blasted with sunshine in the afternoons.

A wall of heat slowed their progress. It was the type of uncomfortable warmth that made a person want to lie down and not move until it passed. Cassidy gathered her hair into a makeshift ponytail. Summer had quickly glided into the Texas Hill Country, driving the temperature into triple digits so early in the season.

"Cassidy? What are you… Why… I didn't think… It's you." A man's voice rocketed through her, making Cassidy startle. Her heart pounded loud and hard in her chest as she turned in the direction of the speaker. Her hands trembled and her throat went drier than the Texas dust.

She *knew* that voice.

Only one person had ever uttered her name that way. Wrapped three syllables in so much emotion, as if her name was a secret—the best secret—his lips had ever formed.

But it couldn't be.

Her eyes landed on Wade Jarrett. Wild light brown hair and dark brows. Eyes a muted green like the underside of a leaf after a storm. A mouth with a constant quirk in it as if he was continuously on the edge of smiling, even when he wasn't trying to.

She gasped and shuffled back on unsteady feet. Cassidy stumbled a bit and would have fallen if Wade hadn't lunged forward and grabbed her arms, steadying her.

Strong. Solid.

"How?" she whispered. "When?" Unable to form a solid sentence, she shook her head. "This isn't real. It can't be." He offered her a reassuring smile but it only made her shake her head more.

Because Wade Jarrett—the man who had been the love of her life—was dead.

She blinked, but he was still there, his touch sending tingles up her arm.

The man in front of her was very much *alive*.

Impossible.

"You're here." Wade's voice was raw. "I never imagined… Didn't think… But you're here."

Her limbs shook as black edged her vision. She forced herself to gulp in some air, but it was difficult to breathe beyond the wave of nausea pummeling through her body. "It's really you?"

Wade nodded. "It's me, Cass."

No one had called her Cass for five years.

A loud sob lodged in her throat as she threw her arms around him. "You're alive. I don't understand. How are you alive?"

Wade hugged her back. "Hey, it's okay. It's going to be okay." Wade's voice was the same soft comfort it had always been.

There had been a boating accident and Wade had drowned in the Gulf of Mexico. A gravestone two miles down the road bore his name. Each week, Cassidy watered the black-eyed Susans she had planted there.

But here he was, back in her arms. God had answered the prayers she had stopped praying years ago.

"Mommy." A small hand pressed against her thigh.

Piper. She had witnessed everything.

Cassidy broke away from Wade quickly, swiping at her eyes. Wade's gaze locked with Cassidy's. He opened his mouth but nothing came out. He looked at Piper, then back to Cassidy. His dark brows formed a V.

Cassidy wasn't prepared for the conversation she would have to have with Wade or her daughter when they realized who each other were. Not yet, not right this second. Cassidy needed her emotions to catch up—

needed something to make sense before she could do anything.

She took a step back, finally slipping away from his touch completely.

They had held a funeral. She had mourned him these last five years. This was impossible.

Wade scrubbed at his jaw. "Mommy? You're a mom." He turned his head, focusing on the horizon.

"I know who you are." Piper bounced on her feet, drawing his eyes back to her. "I've seen your pictures in the house. Grandma has them everywhere. Mom too. All over," Piper said. "You're my—"

"Piper," Cassidy broke in. "Go to the big house. Find Rhett." Cassidy jutted her chin toward the large ranch house where most of the Jarrett family lived. If Rhett and Shannon had been talking about going in the sprinkler with Piper, they were both there. And these days, Rhett's fiancée, Macy, was never too far from him so she was probably there too. Piper would be safe with them while she talked with Wade.

Wade was alive.

All this time.

Where had he been the last five years? Why hadn't he contacted them? Cassidy needed answers.

Piper scrunched up her face. "But, Mom, he's—"

"I said inside." Cassidy sidestepped, putting her body in between Piper and Wade. Made it so Piper had to stop gawking at him. She pointed toward the house at the bottom of the hill.

Piper's eyes narrowed. "I know who he is."

"Now, Piper." Cassidy's voice had never been as

stern as it was in that moment, but now wasn't the time for them to meet each other. Not yet. Not formally.

Piper took a few steps back, putting her at an angle where she could see Wade once more. She looked at him for another heartbeat before she obeyed. Cassidy watched her daughter pick her way across the expanse of green in her little cowboy boots, glancing back at them after every couple of steps. Cassidy didn't say a word, even when Piper was long out of earshot. She watched Piper go up the porch steps and disappear into the house. It wouldn't take long for her to alert Rhett and Shannon to Wade's presence. His siblings would probably assume Piper was confused; they thought Wade was dead, after all. But Cassidy knew they would head outside to investigate. They would be here already if they knew.

Lord, help me. How is this possible? How do I navigate this with Piper?

Cassidy sucked in a deep breath. A drop of sweat skated in between her shoulder blades as she turned to face Wade. He worked his jaw around, rubbed at a spot on his neck. His gaze fixed on the door Piper had just vanished through.

Finally his green eyes found hers. "Piper. Is she… She's… Am I…?" He cleared his throat, but his voice was still completely raw as he asked, "Am I her dad?" He glanced down at her hands, checking for a ring. "Or is there someone else in your life now?"

"She's my daughter, Wade." Cassidy laid her hand on her chest. Until now, she had raised Piper alone, after all. "Only mine."

His left eyebrow rose. Always the left. "You realize in most cases that's physically not possible."

She would confirm Piper was his daughter soon enough, but not until they had a chance to talk. The Wade she had known five years ago had been a troubled young man, who had drowned his problems in copious amounts of alcohol. Even when he had been a teenager, he'd had fake IDs so he could go into gaming halls. Before she let him into Piper's world, she had to find out who he was now.

"You have no idea how happy I am to see you, but five years, Wade. Where have you been?" Her voice shook a little. "We thought you were dead." She could hear the tears gathering behind her words.

He flinched.

"Cassidy." His hand moved as if he was going to reach for her again, but it stopped mid-extension. He curled his fingers in slowly, his hand falling back to his side. His Adam's apple bobbed, and he looked toward the little white chapel. "After all this time, I didn't expect you to be here."

Not an answer. He had always been skilled at avoiding hard conversations, but she needed answers so she could begin to make sense of what had happened. Had he been stranded on some island this whole time? Only recently cured of amnesia? What had prevented him from contacting them?

She spoke each word carefully. "There is a headstone with your name on it a few plots from your dad's." She gestured toward him. "Yet here you are. How is that possible?"

He rubbed his hand up and down his jaw and traced

it down the side of his neck. Blew out a long stream of air as he looked out across the ranch. "I'm so sorry."

Cassidy latched onto his arm, seizing all of his attention. "What happened? It was as if you just vanished."

"That's because I wanted everyone to think I had."

She jerked her hand away and took a step back. "Wait. You…you wanted us to think you were dead? On purpose?" Her voice rose.

He took a nervous half step toward her. "Let me explain."

Her anger flared, hot and sharp. Late to the party, but very much there.

He had willingly forced them to live through five years of lies.

After all this time, I didn't expect you to be here.

His words clicked into place. He had left and hadn't wanted to see her ever again. He wasn't happy she was here. He had wanted her to go on believing he was gone. A hot wave of embarrassment washed over her. She felt so foolish for flinging her arms around him moments ago, for her tears.

Wade didn't want her. Maybe never had.

Cassidy willed strength into her body. She would stand tall and face this man. His lie—believing he was dead—had forced her to become resilient, tough and independent. Now he would have to deal with what he had done.

She lifted her chin. "You left me alone."

"For your own good."

"How could you?"

"Cassidy." He put his hands up defensively. "Please, just hear me out."

"You missed almost five years of your daughter's life." There. Now he knew. It wasn't how she had wanted to confirm his suspicion but she couldn't take it back now.

His gaze dropped to the toes of his shoes as if the brown leather encasing them was the most interesting thing he had ever seen. His hunched shoulders did nothing to stem her anger, though in any other situation they would have caused her ready compassion to spring forward. She waited for him to say something more, to explain himself. To offer some reason that might suddenly make what he had done okay.

As if anything could.

He glanced up, his gaze latching onto her face as if she was a lighthouse and he was a ship tossed in a storm. "I didn't know. If only I'd known."

Cassidy balled up her hands.

She would not feel bad for him. She would not pity this man who had misused and discarded her as if she had meant nothing.

As if she had not mattered.

Surely if he had loved her at all, he wouldn't have faked his death. He wouldn't have let her cry and mourn and grieve for him.

"Why?" she whispered. Tears pricked the corners of her eyes. "Why did you do it?"

Wade licked his lips. His hand shook right before he shoved it into his hair. "I thought… It was for the best, I promise. I did it for you."

Cassidy reeled back. "Don't you dare pin what you did on me. Not this. Not what you put them through." She pointed at the house. At the place where Shan-

non and their mother had wept for months over him.
At the home Rhett had left after he and his father had
fought about who was to blame for Wade's death. The
entire Jarrett family lost their way for a while after they
thought Wade had died.

Cassidy had almost lost herself in grief too.

She jammed her fingers against her chest. "Not after
what you put me through."

"Cass, hey." He gently took hold of her arm as he
stepped nearer. "I'm so sorry. You have no idea how
sorry I am. I shouldn't have—I'm making a complete
mess of this. Of everything."

She yanked her arm away from him. "Don't you ever
say you did it for me again, understand? You clearly
did it for you and you alone, Wade. So you need to own
what you did to everyone."

His eyes widened. "That's not what I meant. Let
me ex—"

She held up a hand. Moments ago, she had wanted
answers, but she no longer wanted to hear whatever lie
he was trying to spin to shirk the blame.

He had never loved her. She hadn't known until this
second, but there it was. For the past five years, she had
mourned a man who she had thought had been devoted
to her. Who had struggled in life but loved her fiercely.

But Wade hadn't.

He had left.

Turned and never thought of her again.

Cassidy closed her eyes as she gritted out, "Did you
or did you not fake your death?"

"It's not that simple."

Oh, but it was.

Cassidy blinked away tears as she opened her eyes and lifted her chin. "Tell me, Wade. Were you held captive for the last five years? Hit your head and suffered from amnesia?" She already knew the answer, but he needed to understand what he had put his family through. He needed to see that he couldn't just explain away the kind of pain he had inflicted. Comprehend how ridiculous any explanation he had to offer would be.

"Was there some tragic reason you were unable to access a phone or computer or carrier pigeon to send a message? No kindling for a smoke signal to tell us you were alive?" Her voice trembled, but she held steady. "Or was not telling us—not reaching out—a deliberate choice on your part?"

"Cass, please." He held his hands out to her, palms up.

"It's a simple yes or no answer, Wade. No need for long explanations. The phone number and address are the same, so that couldn't have been the issue."

"There's a lot more to it than that."

"Just answer me." She ground out the words.

Wade sighed, defeated. "I didn't reach out. It was a choice. I already told you that."

"Then I don't need to hear anything else," she said. And meant it.

He had chosen to let them hurt. To let her heart crumble to dust at the loss of him. To destroy his family. He had allowed them to believe and make decisions based on lies.

Nothing could make any of those things go away. Nothing ever would.

At one time in her life, she had fiercely loved this man. Loved the way his calloused fingers brushed the back of her neck or traced her arm right before his lips found hers. Loved the intensity in his eyes whenever they locked onto her face. Loved the caress in his voice whenever they talked together.

For her, their love had been a consuming force. Something that had shoved the rest of the world away. Something that had saved her from the suffocating pressure her parents had stacked on Cassidy her whole life.

Wade Jarrett had once been her everything, and it had been both wonderful and dangerous in turns.

But Cassidy Danvers had grown up. In the past five years, she had built a life where Wade didn't exist. One where her happiness and success didn't depend on him.

And it was a good life. A life she loved. A life in which she didn't need him at all.

"Please," he whispered.

She didn't know the man standing in front of her. Not anymore.

He was nothing more than a stranger.

One she didn't care to know.

Wade glanced around inside of the small white chapel as his oldest brother unceremoniously propelled him through the building's front door. A large brown dog with yellow eyes followed close on their heels. Minutes into Wade's conversation with Cassidy, Rhett had charged out of the big house and wrenched Wade away. Not that Wade had fought him at all. He was ready for this. For hard talks.

But he hadn't expected to ever see Cassidy again.

Wade ran his fingers nervously over the lump on his throat. Was it getting bigger? The nurses had told him it wasn't noticeable, but it's all he saw whenever he looked in the mirror. The doctor in Florida had told him he had time to settle on a medical team that fit his needs. But the doctor hadn't specified how much time exactly. Weeks? Days?

He was a father.

A father.

He had missed five years of his child's life.

His hand went to his throat again. If something happened before he got to know his daughter... If...

He couldn't think that way.

Wade ducked under the pull rope hanging from the bell tower as Rhett guided him forward.

"You can let go. I'm not going to disappear." Wade put his hands up in surrender.

"Given your history, that's debatable." Rhett's voice was a gruff rumble but a raw edge of emotion was evident too. Wade hadn't gotten to say a word to Rhett before Cassidy told his brother that he had faked his death. Had left them on purpose.

She was right. Painfully so. But there was more to it.

The door rattled as it closed behind them. Farther in, Wade stumbled into the colored light spilling through the intricate stained glass windows lining both sides of the chapel. Wade caught himself on the back of a pew and then wheeled around to face his brother.

It was time to face them all.

Face what he had done.

Own his consequences.

He had thought he was ready but after seeing Cassidy, Wade wasn't so certain anymore.

From the news articles he had read online, Wade knew Rhett was now the owner of Red Dog Ranch. One link he found said their father had willed the ranch entirely to Rhett, naming no other heirs. Figures. As the eldest son, Rhett had been painted in the never-do-wrong light early on in Wade's life. All the Jarretts had played their roles, actually. Rhett as the beloved eldest, Boone as the book-smart son with straight A's and Shannon as the lively, optimistic only girl of the family. The baby girl everyone doted on. Where had that left Wade? Out in the cold, that's where. The only role left had been the rebel, the disappointment.

A role he had filled all too well.

The large dog had seated itself in front of Rhett as if it was his brother's bodyguard. The dog's eyes tracked every movement Wade made, putting him on edge.

"Is that thing going to attack?" He jerked his chin to indicate the dog.

Rhett ran a hand over the dog's head. "Kodiak's as gentle as a lamb, unless I tell her to be otherwise."

Not super reassuring.

Rhett had always been much bigger than him, taller with a wider shoulder span. Slightly intimidating, even when they were kids. None of that had changed in five years. If anything, Rhett was even more impressive now. Rhett's hat was askew and his chest heaved, but Wade didn't think it was from the exertion of charging up the hill. Rhett scowled at him, a mask of disapproval that, in Wade's experience, every older sibling perfected early in life.

Or maybe only Wade's siblings.

Disappointing people was Wade's specialty, after all.

A muscle in Rhett's jaw bunched and popped, then just as quickly Rhett's face fell.

"First," Rhett said, and then he crossed the distance between them so quickly Wade had no time to react. No time to block a punch Rhett would have had every right to throw after what Cassidy had revealed. But no hit came. Instead, Rhett yanked Wade into a rib-crunching hug. Wade hesitated for a second before his hands rose slowly to Rhett's back.

Had his brother ever hugged him before? Not that he remembered.

"You're alive. Thank God." His brother's whisper was rough, breath jagged. "Thank You, Lord, for protecting him. For bringing him home."

The fact that Rhett was praying shocked Wade even more than his hug. Out of the four Jarrett siblings, Rhett and Wade had been the two who hadn't immediately followed in their parents' footsteps when it came to faith. Shannon and Boone had both become Christians in elementary school. A quick search online had even revealed that Boone was in seminary preparing to become a minister, a fact that hadn't surprised Wade one bit.

But Rhett praying as he embraced him? So much had changed.

Wade buried his face into his brother's shoulder. "You aren't angry?"

Rhett let him go. Stepped away and ran his hand over his face. "Oh, I'm livid. You have no idea how much I want to shout at you." Rhett paced. "But you're here. Alive. It's a gift. God's given us yet another gift and

I see that and I'm grateful." He stopped and stared at Wade. "I can't believe you're alive. And you're okay?"

Now's when he should tell Rhett he had cancer.

But the words stayed stuck in his throat, right next to the lump the doctors said needed to come out. If he said it out loud, then he would have to accept it was real. He would have to deal with it and make decisions. He would have to consider what his outcomes might be. All things he had promised himself he would deal with after he returned home—after he made peace. And he would, but not on day one. Wade had only learned about it a week ago. He needed time.

Time.

There was that word again.

How much did he actually have?

Rhett was still staring at him, waiting. Kodiak flopped to the ground and let out a long yawn.

Wade nodded absently and his gaze landed on the window in the front door. He could see Cassidy out there still. She was heading down the hill, her chestnut waves bobbing with each step. Seeing her, he had forgotten to breathe, to think for a minute. He had forgotten his troubles. With her delicate features, deep brown eyes and scattered freckles, she was as beautiful as he remembered. More, in fact. The Cassidy he had left had been a nineteen-year-old girl, still growing and changing. Today's Cassidy possessed the curves and maturity of womanhood and her fierce expression had made his mouth go dry.

Despite her initial shock, she had been confident and commanding, and he had never stopped loving her.

Never would.

He had disappeared so she could have a better life. One without the destructive person he used to be. He would have done anything for her. He had. And none of that had changed.

Good thing she was clearly done with any idea of him, because when she had first hugged him… If she had kept that up, it would have been very difficult to keep her at arm's length emotionally. But that's what he had to do. Wade had to focus on healing the hurt he had caused his family and focus on trying to beat his suspected thyroid cancer and both of those things were enough for any man. He wouldn't offer his heart to Cassidy, not broken and sick as he was.

If her reaction was any indication, she would never want it again, anyway.

"Cassidy's here." Wade dropped down into one of the seats. He had imagined seeing his mom and most of his siblings, but whenever he had let his mind wander to the girlfriend he had left behind—which it often had—he had told himself that she was married by now or had moved on, far away from anywhere he would ever be. But here at Red Dog Ranch? The thought had never occurred to him.

Rhett crossed his arms. "Of course she's here."

Wade pressed his palms together, looked down, then looked up at the ceiling. "I have a kid, Rhett." Guilt burned a hot trail down his ribs. "A daughter."

"And she's a really great kid, at that." Rhett leaned against the pew a few feet away on the opposite end of the aisle. "But you had no part in raising her to be that way. Why not, Wade? I'm having a really hard time coming up with any positive reason you could have had for faking your death, but I'm all ears."

His reasons wouldn't appease his big brother. Besides, right now Wade was far more focused on the fact that he had a child.

"I didn't know." He would not have gone if he had known Cassidy was pregnant. Of that he was sure. "I give you my word, Rhett. I didn't know."

Rhett's eyebrows went up. "Whether or not you knew doesn't matter. You deserted her." He said the words slowly, deliberately. "You opted to step out of our lives for five years and by doing so, you missed a lot. You can't ever get those years back. And you sure don't get to stroll in here and pretend like they didn't happen. You don't get to be proud of Piper when you had nothing to do with raising her."

When Wade decided to return, he had known he would face roadblocks and consequences. He had guessed that it would take a long time to regain his family's faith—if he was ever able to. He owned the fact that his actions had caused damage. Wade had returned because he was ready to do something about it and if he was being honest, he had also returned because he was scared and he needed his family.

But he hadn't known the depth of what his recklessness had cost him.

Wade was a dad.

He had a child. A family of his own.

Whatever it took, he was ready and willing to prove that he wasn't the same man who had walked away from them.

He hadn't been there for Cassidy when she had

been the one he was trying to help by leaving. She had needed him.

Although, maybe she hadn't. Maybe no one needed Wade Jarrett.

He dropped his head and pressed his fingertips to his forehead. "This is so much worse than I thought. And that's saying a lot."

"We thought you drowned. They located the boat you were on. It capsized, Wade." Rhett pushed off the pew to stand to his full height. "Was that all for show?"

"The storm came out of nowhere. Everyone had been drinking." Ashamed of his old lifestyle, Wade looked away from his brother's heavy gaze. His eyes landed on the cross hanging on the front wall of the chapel. The sight of it caused the tightness in his chest to ease. No matter what happened or how his family reacted, God had forgiven him. Wade knew that with as much certainty as he knew he was breathing. God had welcomed him home, into His family...even if Wade's flesh and blood never fully did.

The only reason Wade had made it that night was because he had been appointed captain for the evening, so he hadn't drunk as much as the rest of the party. As his buddies all drowned in the Gulf of Mexico, he had hung on to a piece of wreckage. He had tried to save them, tried to reach them, but the storm had produced gigantic waves and they had been out of sight within seconds.

"A group on a yacht pulled me out of the ocean. They saved my life. That's where I've been this whole time." He finally made eye contact with his brother. "In the Gulf. I've been working as a deckhand for cash and places to sleep." Working on luxury charter boats was hard work and long hours that many people didn't want to do. It hadn't been difficult to find crews willing to take him on. As long as he kept his mouth shut, did whatever the guests asked and put in fourteen-hour days without complaint, they had been happy to keep him on board.

"After all that, why now?" Rhett frowned. "Why are you here?"

Because some of the best thyroid surgeons are only hours away in Houston.

Because I'm scared and I need my family.

Wade swallowed hard.

"Whenever we docked, I tried to catch up on stateside news." Most of his last five years had been spent offshore in the Caribbean. The sights had been amazing, but after the first year he had missed the mainland. "I read about the tornado. There were articles about Red Dog Ranch. About a fund-raiser to help offset the destruction."

"Macy's doing." Warmth flooded Rhett's words. "We're engaged, by the way. Wedding's set for the end of the month. Nothing fancy, mind you. We'd like it to be just family."

"Seriously?" Wade offered a tentative smile. "It's about time."

"Stay on topic." Rhett moved his hand in a circular motion. "Why you're here."

"I dug a little deeper and that's when I found Dad's obituary." Wade looked away and swallowed a few more times. He covered his mouth with his hand. "I missed the funeral."

Rhett's head bobbed. "You've missed a lot more than

that. I'll have to get you caught up on what's going on with Mom too."

"I want to help, Rhett. Help with the rebuild. With anything else that's going on." He moved his hands to encompass the ranch's land. "I'm asking if I can stay here, work here." *If I can come home.* He let out a shaky breath. "But I know it's completely up to you."

Rhett turned so his back was to Wade. He scooped off his hat and hooked his hand around the back of his neck, clamping down on the muscles there. He bowed his head a fraction.

"You can give me the worst tasks. Long hours." Wade rose as nervous energy jangled through his limbs. If Rhett said no, Wade wasn't sure what he would do. He had no backup plan. "I won't complain."

Rhett rolled his shoulders as he pivoted to face him. "And what do you get out of it?"

"Forgiveness, I hope," Wade answered with gut-honesty. "I'd like an opportunity to reconcile, if that's possible."

"I'm saying yes." Rhett held up a finger. "But I'm only saying it because Dad's will was specific on the topic. It says I have to always have a job waiting for any of my siblings if the need arises." He took a step toward Wade. "Understand, I'm not saying yes because *I* think this is a good idea. If it were me, I'd ease back into life here slower." He rested his hand over his heart. "I don't think you comprehend how much you hurt everyone and how difficult this is going to be. I respect that you need to handle this how you see fit—however, I need your word that if your presence starts ripping this family apart that you will be mature and do something to fix that."

To leave.

Wade understood perfectly. They had been better off the last five years without him to worry about. Without the inconvenience that he always seemed to be. He would have to prove he wasn't that troubled boy anymore. The thought stole any desire to share his health news with Rhett. He didn't want them to see him as a burden again, not yet. Maybe not ever.

Wade closed his eyes and sucked in a long breath. Let it out. "I've changed a lot in five years, Rhett."

"Good, because I would love if you proved me wrong," Rhett said. "I really would."

"I will." Wade jammed his hands into his pockets. "I'm not the constant failure of a person I once was."

"You were never a failure." Rhett's smile was sad. "But that's a talk for another day."

They had talked long enough. It was time to head down to the house. To face whomever was there. Wade's gut clenched with anxiety but he started toward the door anyway. Kodiak groaned as she got to her feet and trailed Rhett.

Rhett held out his arm, stopping Wade's progress. "One more thing."

"Sure."

"Cassidy."

"What about her?" Wade tugged his hands from his pockets to cross his arms over his chest.

"Stay away from her."

"Listen, I will be forever grateful that you all stepped

in and took care of her for me, but she was my girlfriend and I get to—"

"Wrong." Rhett stepped so close he was in Wade's personal space. "She is your nothing. You don't have the right to think about her as anything to do with you other than the mother of your child who you will respect. Understood?" His tone invited no debate. "You lost that right when you abandoned her."

Wade straightened his spine. Cassidy and Piper were *his* family—a family he hadn't known he had but now that he did, he wanted to get to know his daughter and be a part of her life in whatever way he could, and that meant dealing with Cassidy too.

He would abide by almost any rule Rhett could toss at him, but not this. However, arguing with Rhett would get him nowhere fast. Wording in the will or not, Wade knew if he angered his brother, the man could send him packing.

"You're right," Wade offered because it was true. "I have no claim on Cassidy." He licked his lips. "I just… I'd like to try… I'd like to spend time with her and Piper."

"That'll be up to Cassidy," Rhett said. "But keep in mind, you don't get to have expectations about what any relationship with her will look like. Everything is on her terms—her boundaries. She does not have to let you into her life again and I wouldn't blame her if she chose not to."

"Agreed." He walked beside Rhett toward the door.

Rhett clapped him on the shoulder right before they exited. "Welcome home."

Chapter Two

Wade stayed beside Rhett as they cut down the hill and crossed the land that had housed the cabins the ranch used for Camp Firefly, the summer camp they hosted for foster kids. Three cabins were in various states of rebuild but the rest of the space was simply outlines where no grass grew, the forms of the old cabins seared into the soil's memory.

"Everyone's been understanding so far." Rhett explained how, despite all the work they had accomplished, he had been forced to shift the summer camp schedule back by a month. Thankfully they had only planned on hosting four weeks instead of the six their father had always organized, but if they had to fiddle with the dates any more, there wouldn't be enough time left in the summer.

"Most people seem happy that we haven't outright canceled everything this summer." Rhett surveyed the area. "I really hope we don't end up having to, after all."

"We won't." Wade let his gaze trail to the other side of the ranch, where the cattle and horses were penned and the metal sides of a new pole barn glinted in the evening sunshine. Rolling hills and a lake in the distance—how had he been able to leave this place? It hadn't been an easy choice to stay away, but each year he had been gone had faded Red Dog Ranch little by little in his memory. Being back now, he couldn't imagine ever leaving willingly.

Wade swallowed around the unexpected emotions the sight had jammed down into his throat. "Like I said, I'll do whatever I can to help." He would be around for the long haul this time.

If they wanted him.

As they approached the family home, the front door swung open and a petite woman charged down the front steps. She started sprinting toward them, her blond curls springing with every step.

Shannon.

Wade stopped in his tracks. A trickle of sweat carved a path down his back as he waited under the onslaught of the Texas sun. He found the nervous urge to trace the lump on his throat. Of anyone, Shannon might notice something was wrong. She would pick up on his unspoken truths. She always had in the past.

His sister had been his best friend. Their connection as twins had almost guaranteed that. Out of everyone in his family, he had struggled the most with wanting to send Shannon a note over the years to let her know he was alive and to see how she was, who she had become.

A note to say he loved her. Missed her.

Rhett cleared his throat. "You realize by now Cassidy has told her what happened and she's just as likely to be running out here to yell at you as she is to hug you. It's a toss-up." Rhett gave Wade's shoulder a small squeeze.

He was good with either.

Wade shot Rhett a quick grin. "She always kept us on our toes, didn't she?" Then Wade turned his attention back to his sister. He started toward her, widening his strides and opening his arms—hopeful she would be happy to see him. When Shannon crashed into his chest, she caused the air to whoosh from his lungs. Immediately she enfolded him in a warm hug. Before she could say anything, she started crying, her shoulders shaking with loud sobs.

"Hey." Wade tightened his hold on her. "I'm here."

"Cassidy told me." Shannon pushed back a little so she could look up at him. Her light blues pinned on his face. "This whole time, where have you been? How could you do this to us?"

He didn't think telling her he had been a jerk would satisfy her. He hadn't called or written and had allowed everyone to draw false conclusions. Worse, he had stayed away, knowing—counting on the fact—that they would wrongly assume he was dead.

"I've been in the Gulf," he said softly. Though he knew that wasn't the answer she most wanted.

She stepped back, finally breaking all contact with him. Shannon fisted her hands. "I am beyond angry with you. At you. I don't think I've ever been so furious with someone in my whole life. What you did to us… What you let us believe—" Her voice hitched.

"I'm so sorry, Shannon. You have no idea how sorry I am."

More than he had ever thought.

Wade shoved his hands into his pockets, willing to take whatever she had to say. What he had done easily earned him a lifelong tongue-lashing. And knowing his sister, she had plenty of zingers stored up to pile on him.

"But, Wade?" She waited for him to meet her eyes again. "I love you. I think you need to hear that more than anything else I have to say right now." She rocked on her feet. "Between losing Dad, Mom's Alzheimer's diagnosis, Boone and his family moving clear across the country and what the tornado did to our ranch..." She used her hand to shield the sun from her eyes as she scanned the evidence of the storm's damage throughout their property. "Our family's been through a lot recently."

Shannon sighed. "Rhett and I were fighting when the tornado hit." She looked over at Rhett and they exchanged tender smiles. "And for a few hours there, I didn't know if he was dead or alive. All that time, I kept thinking my last memory of him, my last moments with him, would have been me tossing a heap of cruel words at him." She laid a hand on her stomach as if the thought made her physically sick. "I don't ever, ever want to feel that way again."

"That had to have been scary."

Shannon nodded. "I learned my lesson though. Which is good timing for you because if you had shown up out of the blue two months ago, before we lived through the tornado and before we lost Dad, well, let's just say this reunion would have gone down a lot differently."

Wade had no doubt.

He had expected much worse.

Rhett excused himself to meet up with Macy as Shannon filled Wade in on some of the plans they had to improve the ranch once the rebuilds from the storm were completed. A part of Wade wanted to go inside and see his mom, but more than anything he was exhausted from the last few hours of seeing people and trying to explain himself. Today he had learned he had a daughter. He had discovered that his old girlfriend was still going to be a part of his life—something he hadn't prepared for. Then there was an appointment in Houston later in the week to meet a team of specialists, which weighed on him too. He had thought he could lean on his family for support but now he didn't feel right expecting that of them, burdening them with what was going on in his life. Not after Shannon had just said life had been so hard recently.

It was a lot to process and he was emotionally wrung dry from it all.

If Wade was being honest, he was becoming more than a little overwhelmed by all he had to catch up on. Lives had happened. People had changed. He had changed too.

Despite those things, Wade knew he belonged at Red Dog Ranch with his family.

He rubbed his palms against his jeans.

He would make this work. He could be the brother and son they had always wanted, instead of the one who had disappointed them. They had urged him to grow up and be responsible, to make the family proud…and maybe he could now. He hoped he could. Because he knew he couldn't erase the pain of the past but if they would let him, Wade wanted to chart the course for a better tomorrow.

"Today's a bad day for Mom." Bad days, Shannon explained, were days when their mom was struggling with living in the past and was more agitated and less understanding. Because of that, Rhett and Shannon hadn't informed their mom about Wade's return when Piper skipped inside to tell them. As much as he wanted to see her, it would probably be for the best if Wade allowed himself the night to recharge and spent time with his mom in the morning.

So he stayed on the porch and listened to Shannon talk about building a covered riding arena, hydroseeding, plans to clear brush for another pasture and a new trail they were considering paving.

The sun was beginning to set when Wade noticed Cassidy near a grassy enclosure housing a donkey and a little white horse. Wade watched her hug the donkey's neck and run her fingers over the tiny horse's back. She rested her head against the fence rung for a long time. What was she thinking about? If it was about his return... No, he couldn't allow himself to hope when it came to Cassidy. He had burned that bridge. He might as well have burned it, collected the ashes and then spread the ashes all over the world—never able to piece them back together or repair them.

In leaving Cassidy, Wade had destroyed the only good thing he had going in his life at the time. No doubt it was a mistake he would regret and pay for the rest of his life.

"You aren't listening to me anymore, are you?" Shannon's question pierced his focus.

"Sorry." Wade shifted to look at his sister.

She rolled her eyes. "It's nothing new. Not when it comes to Cassidy. I wasn't sure you would still get that look about you." She moved her hand in a tight circle, gesturing toward his face. "When it came to her. But you still do." Shannon's eyes narrowed. "I figured you would have fallen in love two or three more times in the last five years and forgotten all about her."

Wade shook his head. He had loved Cassidy and no

other woman. Not that it mattered. Even if there had been someone else, having just sprung the fact that he was alive on his family, finding out he had a child and dealing with decisions about his health, Wade was in no shape to entertain the thought of a relationship with any woman at the moment.

He probably never would be.

Shannon's eyebrows rose. She was clearly still waiting for him to say something.

"It's not like that. There's no one. Not Cassidy, not anyone. I didn't even know she would be here. My only focus right now is getting right with my family." And beating his thyroid cancer, but he wasn't about to unload that news.

"You're honestly going to look me in the eye and tell me you don't care about her?" Shannon snorted. "Five years doesn't change the fact that I could always read you, you know that, right?"

Wade ran his hand over his hair. He laced his fingers behind his neck and squeezed his palms into the skin there. "I have to talk to her."

"About that." Shannon snagged his arm. "When news came that you were most likely dead, it devastated her." Shannon jutted her chin toward Cassidy. "But even after that, she held on to hope. We all did, but Cassidy most of all. Dad poured money into hiring search teams. Four teams in five months and they came up with nothing. Around the seven-month mark when Dad finally announced that we needed to honor your memory and hold a service for you, the stress of it sent her into early labor."

Wade's gaze went back to Cassidy. He swallowed hard.

He had stayed away to help her. He still believed that. But he had also made things worse, at least for a time.

"But she's okay now, right?" Wade dropped his hands to his knees. "She enjoys what she does. I mean, she has a good life here, right?"

Shannon touched his wrist. "She's grown into a strong, compassionate woman like we knew she would. These days, she's one of my best friends. Probably my best." A distinction Wade used to hold but he had forfeited that when he left, like so many things, he was coming to realize.

"Hey," Shannon continued. "She even had that famous country singer, Clint Oakfield, after her for a while."

It might have been triple digits outside, but ice shot through Wade's veins. "She dated a famous singer?"

Shannon shook her head. "He showed interest and probably would have pursued her if she had displayed the slightest hint of any interest back." She shrugged. "But Cassidy doesn't seem to want to date at all. She's pretty happy focusing on Piper."

"Thank you for telling me all this. It helps."

"Nothing I said was for your benefit. It's a warning, Wade. Because while no matter what you've done or how much destruction your choices caused, I'll always love you," Shannon said, "Cassidy is like a sister to me so don't you dare hurt her or ruin everything she's built in the last five years. If you mess up her life here, you won't find a welcoming ear anywhere on this ranch or far beyond."

Wade met his sister's hard gaze. "Understood."

Shannon let go of his wrist and got up. She dusted off her jeans. "Well, what are you waiting for?" She jerked her head in Cassidy's direction. "Get to it. Whatever you wanted to talk to her about. But remember what I said."

Wade took a rattling breath and then headed toward the pasture.

Cassidy sunk her fingers into the soft hair on Sheep's neck. Rhett had given the little white horse to Piper for her third birthday and her daughter had immediately said she was naming the horse Sheep. The name had stuck and it had caused endless confusion among staff and campers when someone went looking for a herd of sheep that didn't exist.

Sheep nuzzled Cassidy's pocket in search of more apple pieces. He nickered. Romeo, the ranch's over-friendly donkey, came to crowd Cassidy's other side. Ever the charmer, the donkey trained his soulful gaze on her.

But Cassidy's focus was elsewhere.

Wade's alive.

Cassidy had lost count of the number of times the words had shot through her mind. She knew they were true, but her heart and brain were having a hard time shaping them into something that made sense. So many choices in her adult life had been made on the basis of Wade being dead.

And it had all been one big joke.

All of her tears, hours in counseling, sleepless nights and days without eating as she grieved. Holding on to his memory, visiting his gravestone, pushing away any other men or even the thought of a relationship.

Every minute had been one big *Gotcha!* on her life.

It felt as if walls were closing in on her heart and a

cord was wrapping its way around her chest, truncating her breaths, making her heart beat out a jagged distress call.

But who would hear her plea for help? Surely not God, who had listened to all her prayers and tears over Wade—God, who had known Wade was alive the whole time Cassidy was in misery. He had allowed her to suffer for no reason. For years.

How was *that* loving?

How was that the kind father who Pastor Ellis often said God was?

When Cassidy had hit rock bottom, the only thing that had kept her afloat had been her newfound faith in God. Losing Wade had been what had driven her to church.

So now—right or wrong—her faith in God felt like part of the joke being played on her too. Cassidy *wanted* to pray like she normally did during stressful times. She wanted to trust and be optimistic. She really did. But she held back.

She held her words and heart away from God for the first time in five years.

Blinking away angry tears, Cassidy focused back on Sheep. "You miss Piper, don't you, buddy?"

Someone cleared their throat behind her. Without turning around, Cassidy knew it was Wade. She had expected him to track her down at some point. Rhett had interrupted their earlier conversation and there was so much more to say.

Not that Cassidy would ever be ready for any conversation with Wade.

"Where is Piper?" His voice was so hesitant, so soft and unconfident. So un-Wade-like.

Some part of Cassidy momentarily wished she was the type of person who could ignore him and walk away without a word. But her friends had dubbed her an eternal optimist—too compassionate for her own good—and they were probably correct.

Cassidy pivoted so she could see his profile. She had always loved his hair, how it seemed to do whatever it wanted and he still somehow looked photoshoot ready. Wade had shunned the cowboy hats both of his brothers often wore. For good reason—why hide a head of hair when it looked that great?

Enough of that.

She needed to focus on being upset with him for what he had put her through, and zeroing in on how attractive he was wouldn't help her down that path.

The fading sun cast his features in shadows. She was glad. It made it easier not to meet his eyes and remember all there had once been between the two of them, what the man before her had once meant to her.

All that could never be.

One man's lies had altered the entire course of her life and dashed all the childhood dreams she had carried for her future. Cassidy locked her jaw. If one good thing had come from the mess Wade had made, it was the iron lock shielding her heart. No man would ever wield such power over her heart and emotions ever again.

Cassidy ran her hand down the front of her tank top, smoothing out wrinkles that weren't even there. "A friend from church came and picked her up."

Wade turned his head and scrubbed his hand over his mouth. His fingers shook a little. "Because of me?"

"They had a sleepover planned already. We just bumped up the timeline a little."

He dipped his head a bit, acknowledging what she had said. Then he shot out a long stream of breath. "I know you don't want to hear this, but at some point we need to address what's going to happen here. I want to meet her. Actually, formally meet her."

"Sure, at some point."

"Really?" Wade's eyes widened.

While she would admit the thought of it made her more than a little uncomfortable, Cassidy would not stand in the way of the two of them meeting. Although meeting and spending time together were two very different things. Piper deserved to meet her dad—deserved to know the truth—and Wade would have to look into his child's trusting wide brown eyes and explain to her why she was only just meeting him now.

Why everyone thought he had been dead.

She had talked to Piper about Wade ever since she was a baby. *Your daddy would have loved you so much. I wish you could have met your daddy.* And Piper had recognized who he was immediately from the many photos of him gracing the Jarrett family home. Not to mention the shelf of pictures Cassidy had in the bungalow where she and Piper lived on the property.

The shelf of pictures she would take down and put away the second she got through the door tonight. Correction: not put away—throw away.

It felt as if the day had been sixty hours long. Cassidy's back was sore and her feet ached. She hooked an elbow on the fence for support. She didn't want to talk to this man. Didn't want to be around him right now, but what would be the point of avoiding the inevitable?

"But don't get any ideas yet. I think I'm allowed a day or two to absorb what's happened, if you don't mind." She summoned all her pain and tears and hurt and let them form a shield between her and him. Because it was necessary to protect herself from his hopeful expression and what it did to her heart.

She stood a little taller. "I've been functioning under the impression that you were dead for a long time. And between you and me, it's a bit of a shock to process." She kicked at a rock on the ground, sending it tumbling end over end until it came to a rest in the pebbled driveway. "Not that you care about any of that."

"I care, Cassidy." A muscle in his jaw popped. His hand came up a few inches as if he wanted to reach out and take her hand, but he hooked it on his shoulder instead. "You have no idea how much I care. I—"

"Well, if this is how you treat people when you *supposedly* care about them—" she whistled long and low "—I sure don't begrudge your enemies."

He shifted his weight one foot to the other. "I deserve that."

"And more."

"And more," he agreed. "But I'd like the opportunity to actually talk to you about what happened."

"Oh, you would, would you?" Cassidy could hardly recognize her voice for the bite in it. She couldn't recall ever using such a tone with someone before.

"Cass." A single syllable spoken so tenderly. But she wouldn't let that change anything.

Wade had always known how to sweet-talk.

Kind, optimistic Cassidy had been easy to trick, to be the butt of his five-year joke. She wouldn't give Wade the chance to make a fool out of her again.

Not ever again.

Something she had learned during the last few years was that being kind didn't mean she had to hold her tongue all the time. One didn't cancel out the other. Being kind did not have to equal being a doormat in relationships. A kind person could speak hard truths and that didn't rob away their kindness.

And right about now, Wade was in need of some hard truth.

"Know what I would have liked?" Cassidy faced him fully. "The human decency of being dumped. Faking your death to get out of a relationship was a bit drastic, even for you."

"I wasn't— I didn't—" He jammed his hand into his hair, wove his fingers into the strands and yanked. "I loved you, Cassidy. I loved you more than life."

His words bounced off the shield she'd constructed from her pain and tears.

She lowered her voice and used a tone she often used when Piper was in trouble. "I think you were young and at one point you might have thought you felt something, but it wasn't love. It couldn't have been."

He opened his mouth, but she shook her head.

"What you did to me? That wasn't loving, Wade. It was pretty much the extreme opposite." She sighed, and if felt as if more than her lungs were deflating. "Love is more than stolen kisses and some whispered words.

It is day in and day out dedication. It shows itself in someone's actions."

And when his actions were laid out on the table and added together, they would not equal love. She didn't need to say it for him to understand.

He had used her and when he had decided she had no intrinsic value, he discarded her.

It was a truth he would never be able to erase. One she would remind herself of every time his gentle, searching gaze fell on her.

Wade gripped the fencing near where she stood and Cassidy wished he hadn't. He smelled like salty ocean air and late-night walks and even now, even after everything, his proximity made her heart rate tick up. It had always been that way between them though—a strong physical pull to one another. Her younger self had confused attraction with love. Physical desire is all that had existed between them, not anything real, not anything lasting.

Not anything worth fighting for.

She realized that now.

No matter how handsome or charming Wade was, she wouldn't allow herself to be drawn to him again.

"I will never be able to take back what I did. I may never get the opportunity to explain why I did it." Close up now, his eyes blazed with intensity. "But when I say I loved you—believe me. What I felt for you was the realest, rightest thing I've ever felt. And it doesn't matter if you doubt that—it's my fault that you would—but disbelief doesn't make something any less true." He took a step back and ran his hand over his jawline. His fingers tripped along his throat.

She hugged her arms to her body. It had been hot all day but a sudden chill rolled down her back. "It certainly makes for a nice story. But I know what happened, Wade. You can't rewrite it into something prettier than what it was."

Wade barked out a single laugh that held no trace of humor. "You don't believe me. You don't want anything to do with me. Message received. I get it," he said. He crossed his arms, mirroring her pose. "Will Piper be back tomorrow? Should we pick a time so I can meet her?"

Cassidy held up a hand. "I said this will happen on my time, when I'm ready. It definitely isn't happening tomorrow."

He frowned. "Then when?"

"When I decide it's the right time. For now, I want to make sure you're not going to meet her and then never have anything to do with her again."

"I wouldn't—" He worked his jaw back and forth, clearly biting back whatever he was about to say. "I'm not leaving. You know that, right?"

"We'll see."

Deep down, she hoped he would prove her wrong. For Piper's sake, she hoped he'd stay.

Maybe for Cassidy's sake too.

She firmly shoved that thought away.

Foolishness like that had only ever gotten her a broken heart.

Chapter Three

Cassidy lifted the stiff curtain and peeked out the window in her small office located on the side of the dining hall. From her vantage point, she spotted a lone figure near the row of growing camper cabins. It was past dinner, past quitting time, but he was still out there.

Had been all week.

For four of the last five days, he had worked from sunup to sundown, and the one he hadn't worked like that he had been gone from the ranch. The first time he had put in a thirteen-hour workday she had thought he simply wanted to make a good impression on everyone. But then he had done it again and again. He worked with every ounce of his strength until he dragged himself to the Jarrett family home each night. Rhett had told her they were now five days ahead of schedule thanks to Wade's dedicated efforts.

She let go of the curtain and watched it fall back into place.

It was the second time Wade had skipped dinner that week.

Without giving her actions much consideration, Cassidy left her office and headed toward the kitchen. Workers needed to eat. That's all there was to it. It didn't matter who he was. Their history didn't factor into her actions.

She automatically snagged a plate from the cabinet, then headed into the walk-in fridge. Cassidy piled a large piece of fried chicken, brown sugar cowboy beans, buttermilk and chive whipped potatoes, and a few corn-bread muffins onto the plate. At the last minute, she remembered Wade had always had a soft spot for seafood so she wedged a generous chunk of pan-seared snapper next to the chicken. She tossed everything into the warmer to heat while she gathered an insulated jug, a mug, silverware and napkins and set it all in a basket.

Back in the walk-in fridge, she fetched what remained of her homemade blackberry lemonade to pour into the insulated jug and two of the caramel brownies she had tucked away for later. She dashed back to her office and picked up a little note scribbled in uneven letters on pink paper. Cassidy's eyes clouded over as she read the sweet words Piper had scrawled there for Wade. No doubt someone had helped her spell out everything, but the giant letters were from Piper's heart. Cassidy prayed Wade wouldn't break it. She ran her thumbs over the paper before tucking it into her back pocket.

When the plate of food was warm, she carefully wrapped it in foil and set it in the basket with some pot holders. Satisfied with the meal, she hauled up the basket and headed outside.

Cassidy was more than halfway down the hill when she started having second thoughts.

What would Wade make of her offering?

She clamped her fingers tighter around the basket's handle. Wade was doing hard manual labor in the hot sun and was no doubt hungry. He would be of no use to the ranch if he passed out or got himself injured. She could set aside their personal baggage because a hard worker not eating didn't sit well with Cassidy. She was the head chef, after all. It was basically her job to make sure everyone at Red Dog Ranch had the nourishment they needed in order to keep up their stamina.

There was zero reason for awkwardness.

She was simply doing her job.

Though she had never packed and carried out a basket to a lone worker before.

Nor noticed who had eaten and not eaten.

Or how many hours one of the ranch hands put in on any given day.

Cassidy straightened her shoulders. She had never noticed because no one else was reckless enough to skip meals. People tended to look forward to her cooking, so she had never had to entice someone to turn in for the day. That's all this was. Her actions had nothing to do with whom she was bringing food to. It didn't matter that it was Wade.

Maybe it mattered a little.

Cassidy adjusted the basket, moving it to rest against her other hip.

The back of Wade's gray T-shirt was wet with sweat as he swung his hammer. His shirtsleeves were the snug kind that hugged his biceps. Wade was stronger than she remembered—much more filled out than the twenty-year-old lanky boy who had kissed her goodbye when he left for an ill-fated fishing trip. The years had chiseled his muscles and built his work ethic.

Cassidy stepped into his line of vision and he stilled. Set his hammer down on the platform.

"Everything okay?" His eyes searched hers. "You okay?"

They hadn't spoken since their conversation by Sheep and Romeo's enclosure. Cassidy had sent Piper to stay with some friends who had kids Piper's age to play with, but the few times Piper had been on the property, Wade hadn't tried to make contact with her behind Cassidy's back. He had respectfully waited for Cassidy to make a move.

"How come you're still out here?"

He propped a hand on the framing he had been working on. "There's still work to be done."

"That's what tomorrow's for."

He shrugged. "If there's still light to work by, might as well keep at it."

"Is this some twisted sort of penance? Because you know you don't need to do that."

He pressed off the framing and cocked his head. "Don't I?"

The question was best left ignored. She didn't need to get into deep conversations with him.

Cassidy lofted the basket. "I brought you food."

He raised an eyebrow. The left one.

"A man's gotta eat." Suddenly self-conscious, she set the basket on the platform near where he was standing. "When you're done, you can leave the dirty dishes right inside the dining hall and I'll deal with them in the morning." She started to turn away but Wade caught her arm in a light hold.

"Stay with me." His voice was a soft caress.

She stared down at the hand on her arm. His work glove was rough against her skin.

He offered a hint of a smile. "It would be nice to have some company."

If she stayed, she could bring everything back to the kitchen afterward and deal with any leftovers instead of letting them be ripe in the morning.

"Alright." Cassidy slipped away from him and turned her attention on the basket. Setting things up, taking care of others, these were the things that calmed her. She found comfort in the simple action of laying out silverware and pouring drinks. She lifted the plate out and started to fill a cup with the lemonade.

Wade tugged off his work gloves. "You don't have to serve me. That's not what I meant."

She motioned toward a relatively clean patch of plywood. "Sit. You've been on your feet for at least twelve hours today." She started to hand him the plate but froze. A patchwork of black and purple blisters covered both of his hands. Some of his fingers had patches of skin that were completely ripped open. Blood had dried along his knuckles. "Oh, Wade. That has got to hurt."

Wade fisted his hands and let them drop to his sides. "It's not as bad as it looks."

She placed his food on the plywood, then turned and seized his wrist. She yanked his arm so she could see his hand but he kept his fingers fisted tightly.

Cassidy sent him her best don't-mess-with-me-I'm-a-mom look. "You either open up this hand or I'll pry your fingers open. It's up to you how this goes down but I win either way."

Wade flinched as his fingers unfurled. A large blister on his palm oozed a shiny liquid. Without a word, Cassidy let go of him and started packing everything back in the basket.

"What are you doing?" Wade's brow bunched.

"Come on." She jerked her chin. "Up to my office." She held up a finger. "This isn't a discussion. Unless you want me to call Rhett out here—and you know he'll give you a piece of his mind and then some if he sees your hands like this—you'll follow me." Cassidy started up the hill.

Wade chuckled and followed after her. "Yes, ma'am."

She led Wade into her office, where she scooped up all the papers on her desk and set them in a pile on top of her file cabinet. Cassidy pulled the food out of the basket again and motioned for him to take the comfortable desk chair. Wade required zero encouragement to dig in. He had tucked through most of the food in the time it took her to find her first aid supplies. She would have to remember to move them to a more accessible spot for the future.

Wade glanced around as he finished the second brownie. "What do you do in here?"

She shrugged. "Menu planning, research nutritional information or recipes when we have people with different dietary needs. And mundane things too—like ordering supplies, updating the spreadsheet with best-by dates, managing the kitchen staff when we have enough people to warrant one. Schedule volunteers for dish crew."

He looked up at her. "I'm proud of you—of all you've accomplished."

"I cook food." She blew her hair out of her eyes. "It's not exactly earth-shattering stuff."

"Well, for starters, you cook amazing food. This—" he pointed at his empty plate "—was the best food I've had in months. You beat out the chefs on most of the luxury boats I worked on." He got to his feet and loaded everything into the basket again. "But it's more than that, Cass. You're more confident than before. You're more *you*—or who you were always supposed to be—if that makes any sense."

How dare he talk like that, as if he knew her, as if he cared. As if he saw her truly, better than anyone else ever had.

He trailed her as she made her way to a sink located near the food-prep area. A sign marked the sink for hand-washing only. There were others meant for food. Cassidy eased the basket from his grasp and set it on the counter. Then she took his hands and placed them under a stream of running water.

"Rinse. Wash well with the soap." She opened a drawer and drew out a clean towel. "Then we'll blot them dry."

Wade obeyed her instructions. He used his elbow to turn the water off and then stepped her way, his hands cocked at a ninety-degree angle as water dripped down his forearms. He looked like some doctor in a TV drama scrubbing in for surgery. She suppressed a smile at the thought.

Cassidy hopped onto the counter and reached for

one of his hands. She gently pressed the towel against it, making sure not to rub or scrape the blisters.

"Thank you," he said. "For everything."

She blew hair out of her face again, then stilled when his finger traced along her cheek, up over her ear. A featherlight touch as he tucked her hair away for her. The trail where his finger had grazed flamed with sensation.

She tugged his hand away from her cheek, setting both of them palm up on her knees so she could disinfect the area with alcohol wipes. Plenty of the blisters had popped, leaving his healing skin open to infection.

His eyes stayed on her face as she worked. "Cass?" He waited until she met his gaze. "I'm sorry. If I could take back everything, I would." He swallowed a few times.

She looked away. "For what it's worth, I'm glad you're alive."

He smiled fully for the first time since he had been back. His eyes crinkled at the corners. "It's worth a whole lot. I was starting to think you liked me better when I was dead," he said.

She turned her attention to the first aid kit and found a tube of antibiotic cream. Cupping one of his hands in hers, she blew on the skin, making sure the alcohol was done doing its job before she applied the cream.

Wade licked his lips.

"When I thought you were dead, I almost lost myself." She was bent over his hand and forced herself to focus on what she was doing instead of his face, which hovered inches from hers. "I almost went off the deep end," she admitted in a small voice.

"Cassidy." Three precious syllables.

"The world's a better place when I know you're still breathing in it," she said.

He sucked in a sharp breath. "Can you ever forgive me?"

She took a minute to answer him.

"You know, just a month ago I was railing at Rhett about forgiveness. Serves me right. I believe in second chances, Wade. I always have." She lifted his other hand and lightly touched the skin before applying some of the antibiotic ointment. "But no one has ever hurt me like you did. What happened… I need time. I can't just…" She shrugged.

His head dipped. "I understand."

Next, she found the gauze. She started to spool it around his hand to form a loose bandage.

He let her wrap his second hand. "Did you know before I left? About being pregnant, I mean."

Her breath hitched at his question.

Cassidy tried to focus on the feel of the gauze in her hand, but she could only feel the warmth of him inches away. Smell a mixture of sweat and ocean and crisp nightfall that belonged to Wade and Wade alone. His presence was undeniable.

Always had been.

"I knew."

"We were fighting so much for a few weeks before the trip…" Wade's words trailed off but his question was evident. *How long?* How long had she known? How long had she kept it from him?

Cassidy didn't owe him an answer. She wasn't the one who had run off. Not telling him right away had been wise. Wade had been impulsive and had always fought whatever he deemed to be a constraint: his family's expectations, the rules at school and anything else looking to tie him down or peg him. When they were young, she and Wade had dreamed about packing up a car after high school and setting off on the road with no plans or set locations in mind. Only to travel, only to be together.

After such a strict upbringing, Wade's carefree approach to life had been incredibly attractive to Cassidy.

But a baby wouldn't have fit into Wade's version of their perfect future.

Just like it hadn't fit into her parents' ideal version of who Cassidy was supposed to become.

She tucked the end of the gauze under another strand and tied it off. Then she let go of him and busied herself with repacking the first aid kit. "I found out a little over a month before your trip."

"A month." His voice was hollow. It held no trace of accusation but was tinged with clear-cut hurt. "And you didn't say something?"

"I was working up to it."

Wade leaned against a kitchen island a few feet away. "That's why you begged me not to go."

She dipped her chin in a nod. "I kept waiting to see if you would choose me, choose to be responsible. And I was afraid."

Afraid he wouldn't choose her if given the option. Afraid he would leave her alone.

Just like he had.

"Everyone tells me she's a great kid." Wade's voice sounded far away. "You're so strong, Cass, raising her on your own and raising her so well. You're ten times the person I could ever hope to be."

"I've had a lot of help." Cassidy slid off the counter so she could tug the note from her pocket. "Speaking of, this is for you."

Wade accepted the note and looked down at it. He let out a shuddering breath and pressed his hand over his eyes for a few heartbeats. A tremor went through his shoulders. Cassidy's heart twisted at the sight. Wade had always felt emotions strongly; it was one of the things she had loved about him. It took every ounce of her willpower not to close the distance and go to him. To hold him. Offer comfort.

Wade had used Cassidy and rejected her, but he hadn't committed those sins against Piper. She couldn't hold a grudge against him for not being in Piper's life when he hadn't even known of her existence. He may not have loved Cassidy enough to stay, but given the chance, he might have loved Piper enough to weather anything.

When he finally took his hand from his face, his eyes shone with tears. "Piper loves Dad. Piper loves cats. Have Dad. Need cat." His voice trembled as he read Piper's note out loud.

Cassidy's eyes burned. "I promised her I'd give it to you."

"Please let me meet her."

"Do you still— I need to know, Wade. If you still drink and gamble like before, if some brute is going to show up at unexpected times, trying to collect on your debts like they used to then—"

Wade lifted a hand, palm out. "I haven't been that

person in a long time. Clean for almost four years now. From both."

She narrowed her eyes. Could she trust him? Past actions told her no. But his eyes hadn't been clouded once in the last week, and Rhett and Shannon had both spent time with him and mentioned he seemed changed. Cassidy could keep putting him off but the truth was Piper was begging to meet her dad. Continuing to find reasons to keep them apart would only end up hurting her daughter.

"Tomorrow," Cassidy said. "You can meet her tomorrow."

"Thank you." He cradled the tiny piece of pink paper as if it were a museum-quality diamond. He dragged the outside of his wrist once over his eyes.

"But I have ground rules." Cassidy opened a drawer next to the sink and shoved aside dish towels to make room for the first aid kit. "I'm present every time you're with her. And don't make her any promises about being a huge part of her life, not yet. Allow me and her the space we need to ease into whatever your being in her life will end up looking like. We all need to be patient about it."

Wade nodded. "That all sounds fair."

"Any questions?"

"Just one." He held out his mummy-wrapped hands. "How am I supposed to function with them covered like this?" he teased. "I smell. I need to take a shower but this doesn't seem conducive to that."

Cassidy laughed. She appreciated him turning the conversation toward a lighter topic. He had always possessed the ability to read when she needed to back away from a subject. When they had dated he had known exactly how to find a smile for her, even on the worst days.

Stop.

He left.

He's not back. Not for me.

He's nothing to me.

She willed her smile to stay in place. "Showering with bread bags on your hands is all the rage around here."

His brow bunched. "You know, now that you mention it, I do recall an incident where Shannon fell from a tree when we were racing to the top. We said whoever reached the top first got the last MoonPie. Mom did use a bread bag for her arm whenever she needed a bath."

Wade trailed Cassidy as she flipped off all the lights and locked up the building. Then they walked down the hill side by side.

"For the record, I did share the MoonPie with her at the hospital even though I won."

Cassidy slipped her keys into her pocket as she walked. "I'll never understand your and Shannon's love for those things."

"They're basically a cold s'more. Who doesn't love s'mores?" He laughed. "Well, besides you, I guess. You still love all the fruit desserts more?"

"Chocolate just isn't my thing." She shrugged. She needed to redirect their conversation. Reminiscing about the past and casual mentions of how well they knew each other wasn't safe for her heart. "Give your hands another half hour and then you'll probably be fine to take the bandaging off." Cassidy wrinkled her nose for effect. "You *do* smell."

"Good old Texas sweat." He winked at her.

"Texas sweat?"

"Take normal sweat and times it by forty and you're about there."

Cassidy rolled her eyes and parted ways with him on the path, so she could head farther down to the bunkhouse she shared with Piper. She would need to call her friend Jenny tonight to let her know she would be picking Piper up bright and early in the morning.

Piper would meet her dad tomorrow.

And with that, Wade very well might become an active part of Cassidy's world for the rest of Piper's growing years. Anxiety rattled around under her rib cage. Cassidy wasn't ready to deal with what that could look like. With what it meant to have Wade back in her everyday life.

Yet tomorrow would arrive, ready or not.

Chapter Four

"Come here, child." After breakfast the next morning, Wade's mom beckoned him toward the chair she was resting in. He had followed Shannon's initial advice and had waited to see their mom until his second day at Red Dog Ranch. When she had first spotted him, their mother had smiled her gentle smile, held out her hand and said, "Oh, there you are, my sweet boy. I knew you'd be back. Come here and kiss your mother."

And that had been it. She hadn't peppered him with questions or admonished him. She hadn't given him the stern talking-to he deserved.

As he hugged her, she had whispered, "Welcome home." And despite Shannon's and Rhett's hugs the day before, it was the first time he had actually felt like he wasn't an intruder on Jarrett property. It was the first time he believed that maybe, just maybe, Red Dog Ranch could be his home.

Maybe one day for the first time in his life, he would fit here.

The Jarretts' ranch house boasted an expansive

downstairs with an open floor plan. The wide kitchen flowed right into the living room his mother often inhabited during the day. A two-story floor-to-ceiling wall of windows in the room allowed sunlight to bathe the whole lower level. In the days since Wade had returned, he had come upon his mom in different states of lucidity. Sometimes she asked him to find his dead father for her. Other times, thinking he was still a teenager, she asked him why he was home from school during the day. But often enough her eyes were clear and she greeted him with joy.

So far, today was a good day.

His mom's nurse sat at the kitchen table, organizing his mom's pills for the week, and gave him a nod as he walked past her. Rhett had explained that after their father passed away, they had hired a nurse to be at the house during the daytime hours and were considering hiring a nurse to be with her at night as well. Two nights so far this week, she had woken Wade up by prowling the hallway upstairs, talking loudly about things that didn't make sense. On both occasions, he had ushered her back to her room and held her hand until she calmed down and fell back to sleep. He had ended up crashing on an uncomfortable high-backed chair near her bed both nights. Rhett's plan for another nurse made sense.

Wade reached his mother and cupped her outstretched hand between both of his. She had always been petite, but now she felt frail—so breakable and precious. His gut twisted. She wasn't even old yet. It seemed cruel that she would start to lose herself at only sixty-six.

Five years ago, she had been fit enough to muck stalls every morning and had still ridden in some of the local shows. It tore at him to see her wasting away like she was.

"Do you want me to help you outside?"

She batted her hand. "It's too hot out there. I like it in here with my view and all my pictures." She gestured toward a wide side table that held at least thirty framed pictures. He spotted a handful of himself as a teenager among them.

Wade stooped to drop a kiss onto her forehead. "How are you?"

She slid her free hand to wrap across the back of his neck and held him at eye level. "I'm the same as always. Here and old. The real question is, how are you? That's what I want to know." She let her hand drop away but he stayed nearby, lowering to his knees beside her chair.

"Honestly?" He shot out a long stream of breath. "It's strange being back. I don't think Shannon or Rhett are very happy that I'm here." He gazed out the window. They had been kind the first day but had kept their distance since.

Cassidy certainly wasn't happy he was back. She tried to hide it, but every time they interacted, he could read her nerves as if she was shouting about them. But bringing up Cassidy with his mom would do no one any good. His mom had a matchmaking and meddling streak that knew no bounds. She would try to push the two of them together again and he didn't want to get into all the reasons why he was presently undateable.

Not that Cassidy would want him even if he was dateable.

"So your siblings need some time. Can you blame them? Don't tell me that's why you're punishing yourself." His mom glided her hand out from between his, only to grasp his wrist and flip his hand over. She traced a finger along the bruises and blisters dotting his palm. "To prove something to them?"

"I'm not—"

She tightened her hold on his wrist when he tried to pull his hand away. "Or is it that you're bent on proving something to yourself?"

"Ma, that's not—"

"Because that's not how these things work, child." She finally let him go. He closed his fingers, covering the evidence of the thirteen-hour days he'd been putting in. "Blood and sweat payments may be how things work in the world's economy but with God, that's not how things are done. You don't prove you're enough by running yourself ragged. You don't have to punish yourself. In fact, you don't have to prove anything. Proving is a by-product of pride, after all."

"Come on, Mom. After what I did, I deserve a fair share of punishing, don't I?" He said it as a joke, hoping to lighten the conversation. It was a common habit he had when any talk entered into deep waters. But his mom had never let him get away with redirecting a conversation. Despite her small stature, she had always been the parent who made sure what she had to say was heard and taken seriously.

"Remember the story Jesus told in the Bible about the prodigal son?"

On one of the other days they had spoken, his mom had brought up the same parable. Wade had used his phone to look up the word *prodigal* later on. It meant wasteful and reckless.

A perfect word for the person he had been. The person who had hurt everyone.

Wade dipped his head. "We talked about it the other day."

"His father celebrated his return just like we celebrate yours."

Wade also remembered that the guy's brother had been angry about the prodigal's return. When Wade had read the story in his Bible before bed the other night, he'd agreed with the brother—the brother who stayed had the right to be upset, just like Shannon and Rhett were completely in the right.

He opened his mouth to say so, but his mom breezed on. "The thing we like to forget is that God knows we are just dust. That's all He used to create Adam, you know. At the heart of it all, we're dirt. It ain't pretty when you think about it that way." She pursed her lips and shook her head. "But God knows that fully and has loved us since dirt, day one. If He knows the dirt in our hearts and loves us, who are we to decide we're not good enough? To punish ourselves when He doesn't? Do you know better than God, Wade?"

"No, ma'am," he mumbled.

"I sure hope not."

Wade's throat clogged with emotion. He would have to think on what his mother had said, turn her words over and examine them and pray before he internalized anything, but they were like a line thrown into a raging ocean, giving him a chance. An offer of hope. No different and no less powerful than the rope the people on the yacht had tossed to him five years ago in the Gulf, saving his life.

Could a person fake their death, hurt everyone they cared about and still find grace? He had come home clinging to that hope, and maybe he would only find forgiveness in his mother. If so, then that would have to be enough.

He had never considered the idea of forgiving himself though.

He couldn't.

He regretted what he had done. Hated that he had put people through such a thing. If he could take it back, he would do it in a heartbeat. His choice had been weak and selfish and wrong.

No one would be okay with him just shrugging off his actions and moving on. With deciding to forgive himself and act as if he hadn't caused some great fallout in his family. That would only create further hurt.

His mom adjusted how she was sitting and folded her hands in her lap. "Now I have something I want you to get after for me. I'm sending you out as my hound dog on a trail. Understood?"

A favor for his mom? "Anything."

"Your sister needs you."

His stomach knotted into a stone.

She tapped her finger on the armrest and leaned forward. "She's dating a man who is no good for her. Cord Anders." His mom spit out his name as if it tasted sour.

"What do you mean *no good*?"

Wade hadn't spotted his twin around the ranch much since being back, but he had assumed she was avoiding him. Sure, the first night had gone well, but even then she had said he had hurt her and she was angry. He didn't expect to gain back the same friendship they had once shared. "I'm glad you're not actually dead" is very different than "Let's be friends again."

"That man says something and Shannon believes it as truth. He tells her to jump, she asks how high. He says she shouldn't be around her family and she leaves." His mom's words came quicker and quicker. "Around him, she shrinks into a person she's not meant to be. He controls her. Won't even show his beefy face on our property."

"When I've seen her, Shannon has seemed happy," Wade said tentatively. He didn't know if this information about Cord was true or maybe something that had happened in the past that was long over. No one had mentioned Shannon having a boyfriend but then again, it wasn't as if anyone had started sharing confidences with him either. He would have to ask Rhett to clarify what their mom was telling him.

"She has been somewhat better since that tornado. I think the thought of losing more of her family—even for a few minutes—scared her a bit. She's spent more time around us since then and seems to be on good footing with Rhett again. But Cord still has a hold on her. Mark my words, that man will try to rein her back in soon."

Wade lifted his hands. "Say that is the case, what do you want me to do?"

"Talk some sense into her. She might brush off Rhett and Cassidy and Macy and me, but she'll listen to you. She always has."

"I don't think my words hold sway with her anymore."

"She'll listen to you." His mom's cheeks were turning red. "I'm sure of it."

Wade pinched the bridge of his nose. He needed her to calm down. "I'll try, Mom. I'll do what I can."

"That's all I ask." She pressed back into the chair and let her head loll in the direction of the windows.

The nurse cleared her throat. "It's about time for our meds, and a morning nap is probably a good idea."

Wade sent the nurse a thankful smile. He checked his watch as he rose to his feet. He had an errand he wanted to run before his appointed time after lunch to meet Cassidy and Piper.

"I'll talk to Shannon when I think I have a good opening. I promise," Wade assured his mom. She nodded and then shooed him out the door.

Cassidy got up from the picnic table and wrung her hands as she paced. She had picked this spot by the lake because while it was out in the open, it was not a location at the ranch where everyone on staff could overhear them. Piper ought to have the opportunity to meet her dad in a safe environment away from people who might gape at them.

She tugged on her shirt, fanning the fabric to allow for airflow. Afternoon outside under the Texas sun in summer hadn't been Cassidy's best idea. They were dealing with enough stress without the elements causing more. Air-conditioning would have been welcome right about now.

Piper hopped down from the bench to trail after her. The pigtails Cassidy had braided and re-braided multiple times bobbed with her movements. "Where you going, Mom?"

Cassidy stopped pacing. "Nowhere, sweetheart.

Sometimes people just need to move around when they're nervous."

"How come you're nervous?"

Cassidy smoothed flyaways back from Piper's face. She had forgotten to hairspray Piper's braids like she normally did. "Just about meeting your dad for the first time."

Piper cocked her head. "But I thought you knew him already? You have pictures of him in the house."

Cassidy choked on a laugh. She had known Wade far too well. "That's not what I mean—I've known your daddy most of my life. What I meant was you. You meeting him."

"I met him the other day."

"Not really."

Piper shrugged.

A figured crested the hill that led toward the lake. Wade wore boots, dark jeans and a light blue button-down shirt. His sleeves were rolled up to his elbows, showing off his tanned muscular forearms. He was lugging a banker's box in his hands.

Piper bounced up and down. She cupped her hands around her mouth. "You better walk quicker than that," she yelled. "Mom says she's all nervous."

Cassidy groaned. Piper was at the repeat-everything stage of childhood. She should have known better than to say something like that to her daughter. If Wade was going to be around Piper more, Cassidy would have to keep a better rein on her words around her daughter. She didn't need Piper telling Wade things he had no right knowing.

Wade's gaze landed on Piper and then skirted to Cassidy, a hesitant smile lighting his features. A chunk of his hair flopped out of place with each step. Cassidy was certain she had never seen a man more handsome than Wade in that moment.

He was only paces away. "Did she now?" He set the box down and then closed the distance to Piper. He lowered himself to a knee, getting down to Piper's level, and leaned toward her. "Thanks for telling me." Holding up a hand, he mock whispered to their daughter. "Because between you and me, the truth is I'm a little nervous too. Glad I'm not the only one."

Piper laughed and popped her hands to her hips. "Well, I'm not."

"Oh, good." Wade rocked back to sit on his feet. "At least one of us is brave." He held out a hand to her. "My name is Wade."

Piper wrinkled her nose and let his hand hang there in the air.

A cow from a pasture beyond the hill lowed and another answered back. The plunk of a fish or frog jumping into the lake seemed louder in the wake of Piper's silence.

Wade's eyes widened. He looked to Cassidy, silently asking what he had done wrong. His light green gaze begged her to intervene. Most of her memories of Wade were of a self-assured and overconfident young man, so seeing vulnerability etched in every line, every part of his expression undid her. Cassidy put her hands on her knees and dipped toward their daughter. Maybe it was too much, too soon for Piper.

"What is it, baby? Do you want to do this another time?"

Wade swallowed hard.

Piper scrutinized Wade's outstretched hand as if it

was a complicated math problem, then she swung her gaze to Cassidy. "I thought he was my dad."

Legs wiggling from the emotional adrenaline pulsing through her, Cassidy put a hand to the ground and dropped down next to Piper. "He is, Piper." Wade was the only man Cassidy had ever been with, so she was sure on this point. Since having Piper and becoming a Christian, Cassidy hadn't even dated anyone else. A few had asked—even the megastar country singer Clint Oakfield—but Cassidy had never been interested. She had decided long ago to devote her life to raising Piper and helping at the ranch.

Protecting herself from further pain and rejection was a nice bonus.

She gestured toward Wade. "Wade Jarrett is your father."

"Then why can't I call him Dad?" She looked back and forth between them. Finally she glared a little at Wade. "Why didn't you say *I'm your dad* instead of *My name is Wade*?"

Wade drew his hand back and scrubbed it over the stubble on his chin, then down his neck. "I—I wasn't too sure what you would want to call me. Given everything, I wanted to leave that up to you."

Piper put her hands back on her hips. "Well, if you're my dad, I want to call you Dad."

Wade looked at Cassidy, clearly seeing if she was okay with this happening.

Cassidy nodded. "Whatever you're both comfortable with is fine."

Piper grinned and thrust out her hand, bright pink cast and all. "Then I'm Piper. It's nice to finally meet you. I've wanted a dad for a really long time and Mom always said you would be a good one."

Wade's Adam's apple bobbed noticeably and his hand shook as he took her little casted hand in his. "It's really nice to meet you too, Piper." His voice was thick with emotion. "I think this very well may be the best day of my life."

Piper scrunched her mouth to one side and looked up in thought. "Know what? Mine too!" She dropped his hand and gave a hop before barreling against his chest for a hug. As Wade wrapped his arms around her, he rocked back a little, bringing her little cowboy boots clear off the ground. They stayed like that for a while.

He set her back down and rose, but not before Cassidy caught him swiping at his eyes. She was too. It was impossible not to be moved by Piper's reaction. Cassidy turned away and fanned her face. She focused on someone driving a four-wheeler in a distant field—more than likely Rhett since it looked like Kodiak, his reddish brown retriever, was jogging near the vehicle—as she collected herself.

"I—I have something for you." Wade's voice made Cassidy twist back around. He dusted his hands off on the thighs of his jeans, looked at Piper, looked at the box and hesitated.

"A present!" Piper bounded toward the box. "What is it?" She tugged up the lid and let out an ear-piercing squeal. She squatted beside the box. "He's for me?" She started to cry. "Really?" A loud wail shook her shoulders. "He's mine?"

Cassidy hustled to where Piper hovered over the box. A medium-sized gray-and-white cat poked his head out the top. His green eyes fixed on Piper. As her cries got louder, the cat licked its lips and cowered into the box.

Cassidy whipped her head in Wade's direction. "A cat?"

"He's really mine?" Piper blubbered the words between tears. "I get to keep him?"

Wade took a half step toward Piper and then stopped and looped his hand around the back of his neck. "I'm sort of out of my depths here. Are the tears good? Bad?"

"You got her a cat?" Cassidy bit out the question.

But at the same moment, Piper twirled toward Wade and launched herself at him, hugging his legs. "I love him! Thank you. Thank you. Thank you."

Wade scooped her up. "Your note said that's what you were missing."

"Now I have everything I dreamed about." Piper put her hands on either side of her father's face. "You're the best dad in the whole world." She squirmed out of his hold and charged back toward the cat again. Piper scooped the ball of fur into her arms, cradling him like a baby.

Cassidy took a few steps in Piper's direction. "Careful, sweetheart. Cats don't usually like to be held like that."

As if to prove her wrong, the cat went limp in Piper's arms and closed his eyes happily.

Wade shrugged. "The people at the shelter said he was friendly and liked kids. I guess his old owners had to move to an apartment that didn't allow any pets and they were pretty sad to part with him."

"I love him so much." Piper kissed the cat right between his ears. "I think I'll name him Cloudstorm. Isn't that a good name? Because his white and gray patches look like different clouds in the sky. And gray clouds are storm clouds. Look at his eyes! He's so pretty." She ran a finger over one of his front paws. "Either Cloud-storm or I'll name him Cow."

"Please not Cow," Cassidy said. Piper's pony named Sheep already caused enough confusion among the staff. All they needed was a cat named Cow strutting around.

Wade gathered the box and they walked back toward the big house together. When they made plans yesterday to meet, Cassidy had been firm about them spending no more than a half hour together so Piper could ease in to the idea of Wade being around. Who was she kidding? The time limit was for Cassidy's benefit. She needed small doses to accept this change.

Cassidy fought the urge to say something snappy to Wade the whole walk back. He and Piper looked so happy, but Cassidy clearly needed to set more ground rules for Wade. If he wanted things to work between them as co-parents, then he needed to understand that he couldn't just spring life-changing things on her without any warning.

Nothing would be more life changing than coming back from being assumed dead, but that was a twist she hadn't been able to control.

When they reached the house, Cassidy told Piper to bring the cat inside.

"Grandma will love meeting Cloudstorm." Cassidy pointed toward the house.

"I still might call him Cow."

"Save that for if you ever have a black-and-white cat," Cassidy said. "Stay inside until I come and get you, okay?"

Piper charged up the front steps with her new cat in her arms but before she reached the door, she spun around. "Hey, Dad?"

Wade coughed a little. "Yeah?"

"My cast comes off soon. Not tomorrow but the next day. Are you coming with us?"

He looked toward Cassidy.

"Only if you want to," she whispered.

His left eyebrow went up. "Morning or afternoon?"

She wondered why it mattered. "Early-morning appointment."

He sent Piper a huge smile. "I wouldn't miss it for the world."

"Great." Piper grinned back at him. "Mom said we could do something in the water afterward. She promised."

When Piper was safely tucked inside the house, Cassidy jerked her chin in the direction of the barn. "We need to talk."

Wade followed along. "Is this about the cat? I should have asked you. But I already thought this through. If you don't want it, then we can keep it at the big house for Piper to visit. No one in my family will care." Wade was rambling. He had always fast-talked when he was worried. "It might even be good for Mom to have a pet in the house for company. Other than Kodiak, of course. But that dog is strictly attached to Rhett. She follows him around as if he were the only person alive. So she's not much company for Mom or anyone else for that matter. That dog growled at me every time she saw me the first three days I was here."

Cassidy latched onto his arm and dragged him at a faster pace away from the house. Each step released a puff of sunbaked dust into the air. Once they were around the corner of the large barn, she released her grip on Wade and pivoted so she was facing him. "You can't do things like that."

"What?" He stumbled a step in retreat, his back crashing into the red barn's wall. "I can't give my kid a gift?"

Cassidy growled. "You can't just buy or bribe your way into her heart. That's not how parenting works, Wade." It wasn't how love worked.

"That wasn't what—"

"Don't you tell me that's not what just happened back there." She pointed in the direction of the lake. "That cat is supposed to smooth over five years of not being around. She's just supposed to hug that cat and forget that you've never been there." Cassidy's chest burned. Fear coated her words. The truth was Piper was at an age where she could easily decide she liked Wade more than Cassidy and wanted to spend all her time with him if he ended up acting more like a fun uncle than a father. If the choice was the guy who gave her presents or the woman who enforced rules and told her no ice cream before bed, every kid was going to pick the gift giver.

"Five years of missing every milestone." Cassidy's voice wobbled. "Not being there to hold her when she used to scream all night because she was a colicky baby, not helping her learn to speak or singing happy birthday to her." She was yelling and it was not like Cassidy to raise her voice, but she found she didn't care. Everyone else treated Wade with kid gloves and she always had too. She wouldn't anymore. He needed someone who would speak plainly and bluntly with him.

"It's not my fault I wasn't there."

"Not your fault? Not. Your. Fault." Her voice ratcheted higher. "You've got to be kidding me. That might be the stupidest thing you've ever said."

"I didn't *know* about her." He took a step into Cassidy's space, his breath mixing with hers. So close she could see the shock of gold that rimmed his pupils, giving his green eyes their alluring glow. The muscles in his angular jaw popped when his gaze connected with hers and she had a sudden urge to forget their fight and trace a finger along the line of his strong profile.

Would she forever be plagued by an attraction to him? If only his lies had quelled that.

Cassidy fisted her hands, swallowed hard and lifted her chin. He wasn't as tall as his brothers were but Cassidy still had to tip her face up to match him. A few heartbeats passed where neither of them spoke.

His chest rose and fell. "I can't be held accountable for missing out on big things in her life when you forgot to tell me she even existed."

She laughed once, harshly. "No, of course not. Wade Jarrett can't be held accountable for any of his mistakes. It's just how you are, right? Mr. Take Me As-Is or Move Along, Folks. Isn't that what you used to say?"

He crossed his arms over his chest. "I also used to be a bit of a jerk."

Cassidy nodded. "A bit?"

Wade sighed. "Okay, maybe a big one. I don't know why you put up with me for all those years."

Simple.

She had loved him.

She had ignored every bad part of Wade, convincing herself the good far outweighed everything else. Despite his past addictions, he had been kind to everyone he met and had always made her feel special. No person encompassed all good or all bad traits—everyone was a mix—anyone expecting perfection from others was living life with blinders on.

But those were things they were better off not discussing.

"This is going to be tougher than I thought." Cassidy pressed her fingers against her temples. "We need to figure out a way to co-parent without stepping on each other's toes or this isn't going to work." And Piper had been so excited; Cassidy wanted Wade to be a part of their daughter's life for Piper's sake, no matter how challenging it was for Cassidy.

Wade's brow scrunched in a way that looked just like Piper's. "Is the cat really a big deal?"

"What if I was allergic?"

"You're not allergic. You had two cats growing up."

"That's beside the point." Cassidy huffed. She'd forgotten he knew all about her. "You can't just give her something whenever you disappoint her. That's not how love works."

"First, let me assure you that I know that's not how love works." He was close enough that she could smell the ocean and midnight scent that clung to him. It must have been the cologne he wore. Whatever it was, it was quickly becoming Cassidy's favorite scent.

"Love is being dependable," Wade continued. "It's cheering someone on even on the worst days. It's being there for a person through everything."

Just like Wade hadn't been.

"Exactly."

He took a step closer. "We both know how much I

failed you in the past but I promise I'm not that guy anymore. I can be dependable. And I'm willing to do whatever I need in order to prove that." He reached for her hand, lightly taking it in his. "I'm so sorry, Cass." He wetted his upper lip when his gaze collided with hers. "What I did to you—I'm so sorry. From now on, I'm committed to being here for both Piper and you."

Cassidy snatched her hand back. "Stick to Piper."

She turned and fled before he could say anything else.

I'm so sorry, Cass.

Good. He should be.

If he thought a couple minutes of smooth-talking would make five years of lies go away, Wade was very mistaken. Yet even as she tried to stir up anger inside her heart against him, the only emotion she found there was fear.

Fear that she could lose her heart to him again.

Fear that if she did, he wouldn't care for her back, just like he hadn't before.

Fear that he would leave.

Cassidy sent a quick text to Rhett confirming that he was fine with Piper staying at the big house for an hour while she took care of a few things, then hurried to her bungalow and fired up her laptop. She couldn't stay at Red Dog Ranch. Not if it meant Wade being in her space. Not if it risked her heart and the safety she coveted. He was unfairly wired to know just what to say and how to act to make her care. Distance was her only ally right now.

This time she would be the one to leave.

Chapter Five

Just after lunch the following day, Cassidy knocked on the Jarretts' front door.

Piper squeezed her hand and looked up at her. "Why don't you just walk in? We always just walk in."

Cassidy shook her head. "Not anymore."

With Wade living in the ranch house, she no longer felt at liberty to come and go as she pleased. The family home was now his domain. And while knocking on the door was odd behavior given that she knew for a fact Wade wasn't inside—she had spotted him working on rebuilding the camper cabins on their trek here from the dining hall—she did it anyway. It was a good habit to get into.

Shannon answered the door. She glanced at Cassidy and then examined the doorknob. "Weird. Was it locked?" She stepped out of the way.

"Mom said we don't walk in anymore," Piper supplied. "We have to knock."

"Since when?" Shannon crossed her arms and raised an eyebrow.

"I think since Dad," Piper whispered.

Cassidy led Piper inside. "You weren't answering your phone."

Shannon ran her hand through her hair and looked away. "I think I might have left it in Cord's car. Silly me." She gave a smile that looked so forced it sent off warning bells in Cassidy's head. But Cassidy had confronted Shannon about Cord before and it always led to Shannon arguing on her boyfriend's behalf and pulling away.

"Are you okay?" Cassidy narrowed her eyes. Shannon wore a hooded sweatshirt despite it being extremely hot outside.

"Fine. What did you need?"

"Can you watch Piper for an hour or two?"

After Shannon agreed, Cassidy went and got Cloudstorm from the bungalow at Piper's request. Once Piper was settled on the couch, playing with her cat, Cassidy turned to leave but Shannon followed her out onto the porch.

"Hold up." Shannon trotted down the stairs behind her. She caught Cassidy's arm when they were on solid ground and made her turn to face her. "You didn't say where you were going."

A bright red car bounced its way up the gravel drive, a cloud of dust in its wake. A man in a suit stepped out of the driver's side and waved at Cassidy.

Shannon's eyes went wide. "Who is that?"

Romeo, the miniature donkey they kept in the front paddock, caught sight of them and brayed a few times. He was always begging for treats and pats. No doubt, he would have followed everyone in the family around like a dog if they let him out of his enclosure.

Cassidy swiped sweat from the back of her neck. She should have worn her hair up.

For the space of a heartbeat, she was tempted to be vague. To tell Shannon it was some guy she was going to go out with and let her make her own assumptions. But it would have been a half-truth and the only reason she would have said it would have been in hopes that the information would make it back to Wade.

To try to make him jealous.

The thought was so ridiculous it squeezed the truth right out of her. "He's just a realtor. I'm going to look at a few places."

"Wait." Shannon latched onto her arm once more. "Come again?"

"I'm thinking about getting a place in town."

"That makes zero sense. You have a really nice house that's free here. Your commute to work is a three-minute walk. Red Dog Ranch is your home, Cassidy."

She leaned forward. "I can't stay here," Cassidy confessed. "I can't face him day in and day out. I can't do this."

Her talk with Wade behind the barn yesterday flooded back into her mind, as did the day before that when she had bandaged his hands. Each time, he had said all the right things and made promises that warmed her heart. The intensity in his eyes when he declared he would prove he knew what love looked like had made her want to go on her tiptoes to kiss him. For a few minutes, she had wanted that—wanted him and all the mess that went with it.

And it was terrifying.

She would not let Wade Jarrett close to her heart again.

She couldn't.

She could commute to work. Find a preschool program for Piper. She and Wade could work out a parenting agreement where he got to spend time with Piper for a few hours each weekend under Cassidy's supervision. But seeing him constantly, knowing he was minutes away every second of every day, it would only grow more challenging.

"You still care about him?" Shannon whispered.

Of course she cared about him. That was the problem.

"He was the first—the only—guy I've ever been in love with. That's all. I'm not still in love with him, if that's what you're thinking. It's just, I have a feeling we always get hung up on our first love a little. Which is normal, right? Maybe it'll be like that for you and Cord if you guys ever break up."

Shannon worked her jaw back and forth. "Cord is hardly my first love." She batted her hand as if she wanted that statement to be gone. "No, I think there's more to it. You're worried. You think you could fall for him again."

He'd been back a little over one week and Cassidy had already almost kissed him. Worry was completely rational.

Cassidy let out a long breath. "I'm being proactive. Your brother is this suave guy who knows how to charm his way to get what he wants. He's always been like that."

Shannon's expression turned thoughtful. "I don't

think he ever intentionally charmed you, Cassidy. I think that really was love."

Cassidy shook her head.

Wade had never loved her. His actions had proven that.

Shannon's gaze tripped across the yard to where Wade was off in the distance, swinging a hammer. "You are not leaving your home because of some boy. I won't let you."

"I don't want to brush shoulders with him every day. I'll fall apart, don't you see that?" She was showing her hand too much, admitting Wade still had such an effect on her, but she needed Shannon to understand. Needed Shannon to let her go. "And it's not like we can force him out. He's family, after all."

"Well, for starters, *you're* family too. So no one is letting you get run out of your home either. Second, you're not going to fall apart. You're stronger than that." Shannon tugged the sleeves of her hoodie down to cover most of her hands. "You're probably the strongest person I know."

Cassidy snorted. "All I've done in my life is cook at this ranch. I've never set out on my own. Never taken any risks. I don't think that's exactly strength."

Shannon crossed her arms, challenging her. "Strength isn't something that you have because of the things you do or accomplish. Strength is a by-product of overcoming things you never thought you could. And you wrote the book on overcoming, Cassidy. You're as strong as they come."

"I'm still going with the realtor." Cassidy hiked

her thumb over her shoulder and took a couple steps backward.

Shannon offered a wary smile. "You do what you need to do today, but we'll talk later."

Cassidy picked her way across the driveway, the whole time acutely aware that a figure in the distance had stopped swinging a hammer and was watching her retreat.

Wade had called it quits a little earlier than usual and headed toward home.

He hadn't seen the red car return.

Not that he was watching for it.

Fine, he might have glanced at the driveway a few times.

Or every time a car came by.

When he stepped inside, he was greeted by his mom, Rhett, Macy, Shannon and Piper. Piper, Rhett and Macy had a board game spread out in front of them and a bowl of half-eaten popcorn. Piper spotted Wade first. She sprang to her feet, hurdled the board game and jogged over to hug him.

"Dad!" She squeezed his legs.

Wade lifted her into his arms. "How's my favorite little lady today?"

She wrinkled her nose. "You stink."

He tapped her nose. "You're very honest, you know that?"

She looped her arms around his neck. "Mom said it's good to be honest."

Piper's words felt like a direct punch to the gut.

"Your mom is right," Wade said.

Shannon caught his eye and motioned for Wade to follow her down the hallway. It was the first time she had reached out since he had returned. He held up a finger, letting her know he would follow her shortly.

He carried Piper back into the living room. "Oh, no. It looks like I interrupted a rousing game of Candy Land."

Macy winked at him. "She's trounced us four times in a row. She keeps drawing the ice-cream cone or the lollipop card, which zips her right to the front."

"Look." Piper pointed at Kodiak, who sat at attention a foot from Rhett. "Kodiak and Cloudstorm are friends."

One of Kodiak's eyebrows went up as she watched Cloudstorm on his perch on the back of the couch. Cloudstorm licked his paw slowly as if he didn't have a concern in the world.

Rhett chuckled. "I wouldn't exactly call it friendship yet. Kodiak got too close and he bopped her on the muzzle." Rhett patted his dog's head. "I think we know who won king of the castle." Kodiak gave a little whine and lowered her chin to rest on the edge of the couch, her eyes never leaving the cat.

Wade pressed a kiss to Piper's temple and then set her on the floor. "I need to go take care of something but I'll be back in a little bit."

Piper grabbed his hand and jerked on it. "Will you play Candy Land later?"

He smiled down at her, his heart flooding with more love and warmth than he had ever thought possible. "As many rounds as you want."

A few minutes later, he headed down the hallway in

search of his sister. He found her in the back den. The room had floor-to-ceiling bookcases on three walls, a leather couch and two recliners. It had been his dad's sanctuary.

Shannon sat on the couch. She tapped the cushion. "We need to talk about Cassidy."

Wade stayed in the doorway. He crossed his arms and propped his shoulder against the door frame. "Who'd she leave with today?"

He had spotted the guy in the suit and wondered all day. His siblings had mentioned Clint Oakfield had tried to woo Cassidy at one point—was he at it again? Wade had no claim on Cassidy; he knew that. But the thought of her with another guy had distracted him more than he cared to admit.

Shannon sighed. "Some realtor."

"She's dating a realtor?"

Shannon's brow dipped into a V. "She's not dating anyone, she's trying to leave."

"I'm not following."

Shannon rolled her eyes. "She's afraid to be around you, Wade. How hard is it to understand?"

Wade relaxed his posture and entered the room. Cassidy wasn't out on a date. He dropped down into one of the recliners. "Obviously it's very hard, because I can't puzzle out why she would be afraid of me."

Shannon leaned forward, her elbows on her knees. "Let's say she starts to care about you or depend on you—even just where Piper is concerned—and you take off."

He mimicked her posture. "I'm not going to take off."

"She has no guarantee of that."

"She has my guarantee." Wade pressed his hand to his chest. "I told her I was here to stay. I'm not going anywhere, Shannon. I promise."

Shannon leveled a glare in his direction. "You have no idea how much you've messed with our trust, do you?"

"Believe me, I do. And I hate that I did that and I'd take it back if I could." He dropped his head into his hands, wove his fingers into his hair and tugged. "You have no idea how much I want to take it all back. I don't know how to gain everyone's trust." He looked up at her, his tone tinged with desperation. "How do I gain back *your* trust?"

She crossed her legs and studied the books on the shelves across the room. "I don't know what it will take."

His eyes and chest burned as he considered all he had lost. "I love you, Shannon. I thought about you and Cassidy every day."

"We thought about you too." She swiped at her eyes. "But it was because we thought you were gone. It's so different than you missing us."

Wade pinched the bridge of his nose and closed his eyes. *Help me, Lord. Please.*

"What can I do? Tell me what to do."

"Just get her to stay," Shannon said. "She belongs here."

Wade nodded. "I'll try."

Gaining his twin's trust was going to take more than convincing Cassidy to stay at Red Dog Ranch. It would cost him being vulnerable. Since his actions were to blame for the deterioration of their relationship, he knew it was on him to take the first steps. To trust her. To let someone in.

To be honest about what he was going through—even if it was scary.

There was the risk that she would pull away even more once she knew what he was facing. *Cancer* was a daunting word in any situation. But it was a risk he would have to take if he wanted to repair the damage he had caused.

He would tell her tomorrow.

Wade cleared his throat. "It might be the worst time to ask this of you, but I need a favor."

Her eyes met his and he saw tears swimming in them. It took all his self-control not to get up and hug her.

"I need to drive to Houston tomorrow afternoon for something. There's something I'm going through that I could use some support with. I'll explain in the car." He touched his throat and just as quickly let his fingers fall into his lap. "Will you come with me? It would mean a lot if you did."

She studied her nails. The floor. He thought she wasn't going to answer him.

"I was supposed to go out with Cord," she said. "But yes, if you need me, I'll go with you. It's a long drive to do alone." More than six hours, round-trip.

Wade and Shannon rejoined everyone in the living room. Macy informed them that Cassidy had called Rhett's phone after she remembered Shannon had misplaced hers and had asked if it was okay for Piper to be there a little longer. They had told Cassidy to stay out as long as she wanted. Shannon pulled a chair close to their mom and Wade joined Piper on the floor for his promised rounds of Candy Land. Cloudstorm had plunked himself in the center of Kodiak's large dog bed and was out cold. Kodiak stared at the cat from a few feet away, clearly disgruntled.

Macy scratched behind Kodiak's ears. "Poor girl. That mean old cat just won't give you a break tonight."

Piper crossed her arms, pouting. "Cloudstorm is *not* mean. He's my friend."

Rhett smiled. "She's just kidding, sweetheart." He extended his hand to Macy and when she took it, he pulled her snug against his chest and whispered something that caused Macy's cheeks to flame. "My soon-to-be bride and I are going to head out for a walk." He winked and called Kodiak to follow them outside.

Wade helped Piper pack the game away and then she asked if they could watch a show. He found a cartoon channel on the television and she curled up beside him on the couch. He wrapped his arm around her and she was snoring softly within minutes.

Just after seven o'clock, Cassidy knocked on the door. Wade made a move to slip away from Piper, but Shannon held out a hand, silently telling Wade to stay put so he wouldn't wake her up. His sister went and opened the door.

Shannon pointed toward Wade and Piper on the couch for Cassidy's benefit. "I still need to shower and get a few things done, so I'm going to head upstairs. We had a lot of fun tonight. We should do this again soon but with you here too." She hugged Cassidy and then headed up to her room.

Cassidy clutched her purse to her stomach as she

entered the living room. "I guess we can go ahead and wake her. Her bedtime is always between seven and seven thirty, so she's right on schedule."

Wade carefully scooped Piper into his arms. "No need," he whispered. "Open doors and lead the way and I'll carry her to your place."

"It's a long walk."

Not more than three minutes.

Piper was all of forty pounds. "I'll be fine."

On the way to Cassidy's, his boots crunched on the path that snaked from the family home to the row of staff houses. He wanted to ask Cassidy about her day. He wanted to bring up what Shannon had said and beg her not to move away. But he swallowed all his questions in favor of silence for Piper's sake.

Cassidy eased open the door to the one-story home she and Piper shared. She led Wade through a family room full of mismatched furniture and into a hallway with three doorways. The first was a bathroom. Cassidy pushed open the second door to reveal Piper's room, which was awash in purples and pinks. Her bedspread had dancing woodland animals all over it and a hoard of stuffed animals lined the wall. Wade moved to set Piper down but she stirred, her hands grabbing hold of his shirt collar.

"Don't go, Daddy," she muttered.

He wanted to tell her he would never leave her. He would always be around. Forever a part of her life. That even though they just met, she had quickly become one of the most important people in his life. A wave of sadness threatened to pull him under as he thought of all the missed days and moments. Everything running away, being a coward had cost him.

Wade forced words past the lump of emotion lodged in his throat. "I'm here, baby girl."

Piper blinked a few times, trying to focus on him. "Will you stay and pray before bed?"

Cassidy laid a hand on Piper's arm. "Since you're up, how about we brush our teeth and get some pj's on?" Cassidy eased Piper away from Wade and steered her toward the hall.

Piper stumbled sleepily across the floor. She grabbed the doorjamb before Cassidy could usher her away completely. "You'll be here when I come back from the bathroom, won't you? You'll pray for bedtime?"

Cassidy set her hand on top of Piper's head. "Sweetheart, your daddy isn't a very religious person so we shouldn't—"

Wade got to his feet. "Actually, most people consider me pretty religious these days. If that's the term we're going with." He looked at Piper, wanting both her and Cassidy to know exactly where his heart was when it came to God and eternity. "I'm a Christian and I love Jesus so much, but your mom is right. That wasn't always the case. I'd be honored to pray with you tonight if that's okay with your mom." He moved his gaze to include Cassidy.

"We'll—we'll be right back, then." Cassidy's voice shook.

In the few minutes they were gone, Wade spotted three old photographs of himself in different places in Piper's room. He picked one up. It was an image of him and Cassidy in the stands at their high school's homecoming game his senior year. His arm was slung around her shoulders. She was smiling at the camera but all of his attention was trained on her. He was grinning at Cassidy as if she was the greatest treasure in the world. And she had been.

She still was.

Cassidy cared deeply about others. She was hard-working and loyal and believed the best of everyone to the point where people who knew her were inspired to be and do better. Wade had fallen for her initially because she had seen potential in him and had cheered him on when all anyone else had seen was a disappointment. And more recently, he had hurt her and yet she had been the first to reach out. She had bandaged his hands when he hadn't deserved her consideration. She had let him into Piper's life when she had had every right to blockade him.

Despite all the travels and adventures Wade had experienced, Cassidy was still the best person he had ever met. He set the picture back in its spot on the dresser.

Piper charged back into the room in pajamas featuring cats reading books and drinking coffee. They'd forgotten Cloudstorm back at the big house, but he could run the cat home later. Piper hopped into her bed and thrust one of her hands into his face. He took it and then got down on his knees beside her bed.

"How do you usually do this?" he asked Piper. "Do we pray together or do you want me to pray?"

Still holding tightly to his hand, she flopped back against her pillows. "You pray but I help with the Amen part."

"Sounds like a plan." Wade smiled.

Cassidy appeared beside him and took Piper's other hand. She sat on the edge of the bed, so close her knee brushed his shoulder. A feeling of belonging, of being home rushed through Wade, and it was so strong and unexpected he struggled to keep his breathing even.

"Dear Lord, thank You for today and for time together. Thank You for our family and our home here. You take such good care of us. We pray for good dreams and a great night of rest, so we can wake up healthy and ready to do what You need us to do tomorrow. In Jesus' name, we ask all these things." He paused to let Piper say Amen.

Piper squeezed his hand. "And thank You for bringing Daddy home. I like him even more than Cloudstorm and that's a lot. Amen!"

"Sleep well, Piper." Wade bent close and kissed her cheek. "I love you," he whispered. Cassidy followed, kissing Piper's other cheek.

"Love you guys too." Piper closed her eyes and snuggled into her pillow as Cassidy drew her blankets to her shoulders.

Wade got to his feet. It wasn't that late, but it was darker in Piper's room than he had realized. Cassidy must have hung blackout curtains in here. He placed a hand on the small of Cassidy's back and guided her into the hallway. He eased Piper's door shut behind them.

Cassidy headed straight to the front door and walked outside, so he followed her. When she turned to face him, there were tears rolling down her cheeks. Wade's heart clenched. It tore him up to see her upset. He pulled her into a hug and her head went to the place it always had where her breath warmed his throat. He leaned his cheek against the top of her head and rubbed a slow circle on her back. She didn't wrap her arms around him, but her fingers fisted into his shirt. They stood there for a minute, breathing together.

Just as quickly, she stiffened. Releasing his shirt, she put her palms against his chest and lightly shoved. He let her go right away. She tripped in her rush backward, so Wade grabbed hold of her shoulders, steadying her.

"Hey," he whispered. "What's wrong?"

Tears still fell as Cassidy lifted her chin. "I'm fine."

His thumbs traced back and forth on her shoulders. She felt so small. "Talk to me, Cass. Why'd you look at places in town today?"

She shook her head.

"Please tell me why you're crying."

He wanted to wrap her in his arms again and protect her from whatever had upset her, but if he was the cause of her distress, proximity wouldn't be welcomed. With that thought in mind, he slipped his hands away.

"Like I said." Her voice trembled. "I'm fine."

"My friend Preach has a theory that those two words make up the most often told lie in the world."

She reached her hand back and fumbled for the doorknob. "Well, you'll have to accept them because you don't deserve my truth." Then she turned and went inside, closing the door behind her.

Wade stared at the door, clenching and unclenching his hand. It felt wrong to leave things how they were between them. Seeing Cassidy cry and not being able to fix it felt like a knife to the chest.

She's afraid to be around you.

Remembering Shannon's words finally got Wade to

turn and leave. The last thing he wanted was to scare Cassidy off, even though he couldn't figure out what had gone wrong. Praying with Piper, tucking her in with Cassidy had been one of the best moments, the best feelings he had ever had.

Early tomorrow morning, he was supposed to meet Cassidy and Piper to get Piper's cast removed. He prayed Cassidy would be willing to talk then.

Chapter Six

Cassidy buckled Piper into her car seat, then rounded the car to get in on the driver's side. Jamming the keys in the ignition, she decided she wouldn't wait for Wade if he was even a minute late.

Half of her hoped he would be late. The other half desperately didn't.

Cassidy pressed her forehead against the steering wheel.

Wade had changed. He said he was a Christian now and he was hardworking and dedicated to his family. Since being back, Wade had devoted himself to helping rebuild the ranch and she hadn't heard him complain or get discouraged once. The old Wade would have gotten sick of pitching in after day two without fanfare and praise from his family. But the Wade that had returned seemed quietly content to pour his heart into things without recognition.

Rhett said they were now a week ahead of the rebuild schedule and while they wouldn't have all the cabins back up and running in time, with some shuffling, they would have enough ready to move forward with the up-coming first week of camp.

She had never been more attracted to a man than last night when Wade helped tuck Piper in. After he left, she wondered what would have happened if she had hugged him back, if she had clung to him like she had wanted to instead of pushing him away.

What was wrong with her?

Cassidy groaned.

Wade—even this new version—would only hurt her in the end. She wasn't the carefree teen Wade had known and been attracted to. The years had toughened her and made her cautious. She would never be the girl who could jump in a car and go on an unplanned trip like he had said he wanted. Besides, even back then he had chosen to fake his death instead of facing her. She couldn't forget that.

Piper kicked the back of the passenger's seat. "You tired, Mom?"

Cassidy lifted her head and rolled her shoulders. "I didn't sleep well last night. But I'm okay."

Not only had Wade been on her mind but she had been weighing the pros and cons of moving from the Jarrett property. Sticker shock over housing prices had hit her hard. It wasn't wise to dump so much money into their living expenses when it was all included with her position at the ranch. That money was better saved for Piper's future, for college one day or whatever her dream would be. By morning, Cassidy had decided against moving away from Red Dog Ranch.

Besides, Shannon was right. Cassidy wasn't about to let a guy chase her away from her home. Even one as dangerous as Wade. She would be smarter, would protect her heart better than she ever had in the past. She could live by him and not fall for him.

Never again.

Right on time, Wade's car came up the driveway and parked next to hers. She had expected him to come from the house and couldn't help wondering where he had gone so early in the morning. He hopped out of his vehicle and climbed into the passenger seat all while juggling a large white paper bag and a drink carrier.

"Morning. How are my two favorite ladies?" He twisted in his seat to grin at their daughter. "Your cat slept with me last night. He snores."

"It's cute." Piper shrugged.

"If you say so." He tipped his chin. "Ready to get that cast off?"

Piper groaned dramatically. "Like ten hundred days ago."

Wade tugged the smallest cup from the carrier. "Well, maybe this will make it better." He handed it to Piper. "It's hazelnut chocolate milk. Tell me that doesn't sound amazing? I was tempted to get one myself."

Piper squealed a thank-you right before taking a long sip from the straw.

Wade turned his devastating smile on Cassidy and lowered his voice. "I figured not something hot for her. I didn't know if kids her age drink hot things or if that would be bad in the car so—"

"It was a perfect choice. Thank you." Wade must have woken up at least an hour and a half before them to get ready, run to town, buy goodies and be back in time to leave. Touched by how thoughtful he had been, Cassidy blinked back a sudden prick of tears. "We rushed out of the house and didn't get a chance to grab something."

Wade passed a cup her way. "White mocha. You used to love those so…" He shrugged and tucked his own cup into one of the holders situated between their seats.

"Still my favorite," she admitted. It felt like forever since she had been able to enjoy one. She was usually too tied up with her responsibilities in the mess hall to have time to go out for a fancy coffee drink. Thankfully she'd talked to Rhett about taking some time off before the camp sessions began. With everything going on in her personal life, Cassidy felt like she needed more dedicated time with Piper and more time to process.

"And—" Wade lofted the bag "—big days call for donuts. At least, that's my motto. I'm thinking of embroidering it on a pillow or a wall hanging or something, I feel that strongly about it." He fished a heart-shaped donut from the bag for Piper. It had been dipped in pink frosting and was covered in sprinkles. "This one was called a pink party donut and, let's be serious, I was hardly going to pass up something like that." He reached into the bag again and handed Cassidy a large glazed donut with something shiny and yellow in the middle instead of a hole. "It's a peach pie donut," he whispered conspiratorially. "Satisfies that whole baked fruit obsession you have."

Cassidy immediately closed her eyes when she sank her teeth into the donut. It tasted almost exactly like the homemade peach pies she baked in the dining hall—but even sweeter. "This. Wow. This is amazing."

"Mine's the best." Piper polished off her last bite. "I could eat these forever. Or like a hundred of them."

Wade offered them both napkins before digging back in the bag for a cake donut drizzled with chocolate glaze. Cassidy opened her mouth to tease him about his choice but closed it just as quickly, moving the car into Drive at the same time.

"What? I saw that look." Wade took a sip from his cup. "No fancy stuff here. I'm a simple man."

"Hardly." Cassidy steered her car down the driveway and out onto the country road. She hit the Play button on her radio and it linked to the streaming app on her phone. A song from a Disney movie flooded through the speakers and Piper joined in instantly, singing with loud abandon. Wade glanced back at her and then caught Cassidy's eye and grinned.

"A good pair of lungs on that one." He fiddled with her speaker settings, sending the sound toward the back so it wasn't nearly as loud up front. "Are we okay?" he asked. "You and me? Last night. I was worried, Cass."

Cassidy peeked at Piper in her rearview mirror. Their daughter bobbed and swayed with the music as she looked out the window, clearly distracted and oblivious to the fact that her parents were talking.

Cassidy knew she would be well within her rights to snap at Wade or refuse to talk, but what good would that do? Sure, it would make her feel powerful for a few minutes but hurting someone or seeing them squirm had never been her style. Most of the time, she went out of her way to be positive and smooth things over.

Besides, they should be civil for Piper's sake. That's why she would talk.

Who was she kidding? She had never been known to hold her thoughts.

"It's just a lot, Wade. All of this. I'm not sure how I'm supposed to process or act." She turned onto the next street, which brought the cemetery into view. Cassidy tightened her hold on the wheel while a wave of nausea rocked through her. "I mean, there's a gravestone with your name on it in there." She gestured toward the graveyard. "But here you are. That's messed up."

Wade touched the window, his gaze fixed on the cemetery. "If I could take it back. If I could take all the pain I caused away—"

"But the thing is, you can't." She sighed. "It's a nice sentiment but saying that doesn't make everything we've been through go away. It's all still there like some overstuffed pot of chili on a forgotten burner, getting ready to explode everywhere."

"Talking in food terms. It suits you." The statement could have been taken as mocking, but not how Wade said it. His voice was bathed in so much warmth and pride. As if he cared and wanted to understand how her mind worked—as if he liked knowing this new piece about her personality that hadn't been there when they dated.

"Well, that's what makes sense right now. My emotions are all over the place, and they have to be dealt with but I don't know how. And I just really don't want the chili to explode, you know? I don't think I can handle one more thing." She shook her head. "And no one out there has written any self-help books for people dealing with an ex they thought was dead. Shocking, I know."

"There is a book," he said quietly.

"You're kidding me." She had actually searched the internet for blogs or articles that could help her but the keywords kept leading her to purchase pages full of weird books about zombies or costumes.

He ran his hand over the side of his face. "In the Bible it says God goes before us. He's with us and won't fail us and He won't forsake us or leave us dismayed. That's a paraphrase, of course. I'm trying to be better about memorizing that stuff but it's been slow going." He shifted in his seat to face her more. "What I mean to say is, God's pretty clear that if we need rescue or help or a hiding place, He's there waiting to meet those needs."

Wade Jarrett was quoting the Bible and giving her godly advice. The image didn't compute with the man she thought she knew. Moreover, she didn't feel safe going to God right now. She had run to Him for the past five years and God had played along—knowing Wade was alive while she cried and prayed. But there wasn't enough time left in the trip to get into all that.

Cassidy glanced at Wade but quickly trained her eyes back onto the roadway. "Who *are* you?"

He let out a puff of air that sounded like it wanted to be a laugh. "Same guy I've always been. I just have God's grace now." He leaned toward her. "I want to help. I want to be there for you if you'll let me. Last night, with Piper at your house… Cassidy."

Oh, there was the soft way he said her name as if each syllable was precious to him.

Cassidy swallowed hard. "Do you know how many nights I've tucked her in and pictured what it would

have been like if you had been with us? I've cried myself to sleep plenty over stuff like that. Can you understand what that's like?"

He tentatively reached over and gently placed his
hand on her leg. "I'm so sorry."

"It hurts, Wade. It hurts and it's hard, but then I feel
like it's wrong to feel that way. I have this grief about
all the things Piper has missed out on. But you didn't
know about her and it's my fault you didn't know, so
I'm to blame for the missed time."

His hand was still resting on her leg, warm and reassuring. "Don't say that. You aren't to blame for any
of this."

But he was simply being nice because she was to
blame, wasn't she?

If she had been honest with him before he left on
the fishing trip, their lives might have all been different. Piper could have always known her father. A knot
formed in Cassidy's chest.

Piper's singing grew even louder.

Cassidy turned into the parking lot and found a parking space. Once the car was in Park, she unbuckled her
seat belt and pivoted in her seat, causing his hand to slip
away. She looked at Wade. "I know you wouldn't have
stayed for me but you might have for her."

"Cassidy." Frustration laced his voice, not with her
but almost with himself, with a situation he couldn't fix.
"I loved you." He glanced back at Piper as if to make
sure she was still paying more attention to her music
and dance moves than to her parents.

Cassidy's heart rattled inside her chest. She wasn't
sure she wanted to hear whatever Wade was trying to

say. Hadn't she already decided just that morning that getting close to him was dangerous?

Wade continued, "I know you don't believe that and you have every right not to. But that's the truth and it kills me to think of you believing some lie about what was between us. That first day, you didn't want me to talk about why I left but—"

"Here we are." Cassidy hit Stop on the stereo. She looked back at Piper. "Let's get that cast off." She exited the car as quickly as she could.

She had let her guard down with Wade again and while she knew she had to talk with him in order to heal in a healthy way, she could only handle it in small doses. Anything more and she didn't trust herself to behave or speak rationally.

Anything more and she might believe he still loved her.

Wade held Piper's hand on the way out of the doctor's office. She had kept a stiff upper lip the whole time the doctor used the noisy cast saw on her arm, then declared it only tickled her skin a little afterward.

Piper swung on his forearm as if he were a jungle gym. "Look at how strong I am!" She beamed up at him when she set her feet back on the ground. "Uncle Rhett says I'm the strongest cowgirl he knows."

Wade chuckled. "Well, Uncle Rhett *is* pretty smart." He pressed through the door and then tugged Piper to a stop to wait for Cassidy, who was finishing at the desk in the doctor's lobby. She hiked her purse onto her shoulder and faced them but her gaze didn't meet Wade's.

The talk in the car had been too much for her, but it was impossible for him to sit there and listen to her say she believed he had left to get away from her.

Nothing could have been further from the truth.

He disappeared to save her. He disappeared *because* he loved her.

After today, once the doctor confirmed whether or not the biopsy showed cancer, Wade would know how to proceed with Cassidy. But he had to deal with his health first. He shouldn't expect deep talks with her until he was able to be completely open about everything on his end. And he couldn't tell her what he was facing, not yet. Cassidy had said she was dealing with too much already, so he was glad he hadn't mentioned it to her.

The last thing he wanted to do was add another burden onto her shoulders. Not when he had caused her a lifetime's worth of grief already.

Wanting to sleep in, Shannon had promised to meet him in the parking lot so they could get on the road to Houston. He shielded his eyes as he scanned the parking lot. When he spotted a truck from the ranch, Shannon honked the horn once and climbed out. She was wearing a baggy sweatshirt and jeans, which struck Wade as odd given how hot it was, but maybe she had the air-conditioning cranked.

Piper let go of his hand. "Is Aunt Shannon coming swimming too?"

"I'm sorry, buddy. Shannon and I won't be able to swim with you guys today," Wade said. Piper's bottom lip jutted out and trembled. Wade got down on one knee and took her shoulders in his hands. "Hey, how about tomorrow we go on an adventure together?"

Piper's eyes narrowed. "You promise?"

"Promise." He hugged her.

"Will you be back for dinner? Mom's making steak tacos and they're so good."

"I'm planning on it. Have fun today, okay?"

She hugged him a second time and then jogged to see Shannon. Wade started after her but Cassidy clamped onto his arm, pulling him up short.

"Don't ever promise her something if there is even the slightest chance you might cancel." Cassidy's voice was a low rumble. "It's better to surprise her than to disappoint her."

It stung to know how little Cassidy thought of him and his promises. How little she believed his word meant. Wade shoved away the thick tang of discouragement that seemed to coat his insides. He had lost the right to be believed and believed in a long time ago.

He might never get it back.

Wade set his hand on top of Cassidy's. "Trust me. I'll plan a great day."

She looked down at where their hands touched but instead of slipping away, her fingers tightened against his arm. "You don't know everything she needs or how to work her car seat. You don't know what to pack if—"

He squeezed her hand. "Come with us."

Wade was shocked when she easily agreed. They settled on a meeting time for the next day before everyone parted ways.

"Sure you don't want to go swimming?" Piper called one last time while Cassidy was buckling her into her car seat.

"Believe me, I'd much rather be doing that than what

I have to go take care of." Wade waved as he headed for the truck. "You ladies have fun."

Wade pulled the direction app up on his phone when he climbed behind the wheel of the truck. While Shannon buckled up in the passenger's seat, Wade adjusted the visor to keep the sun from blasting him in the face, then steered the truck toward the I-10.

Shannon fished a bag from the back seat.

"Alright, we have two kinds of chips." She hauled snacks from the bag, showing a red bag and a blue bag. "Peanut butter M&M's, because they're clearly the best."

"No argument."

The plastic bag rustled again. "And MoonPies."

"You found some? I didn't know they still made them." Wade hadn't eaten one in years. They didn't exactly stock them in Caribbean grocery stores. "I *have* to have one of those first." He held out his hand while she unwrapped one of the sweets for him.

Shannon licked a smear of chocolate from her finger. She stretched out her legs, crossing her ankles. "Now's the part where you tell me what's so important in Houston."

Wade swallowed hard. How to tell her? Blunt. Quick. Like ripping off a Band-Aid. "The University of Texas MD Anderson Cancer Center. That's what's in Houston."

She shot up in her seat. "Wait. Cancer. Did you say cancer? Wade?"

Where to start?

He braced his elbow against the window, steering with his left hand. He scrubbed his right hand over the side of his neck and jaw. "A few months ago, I slipped on a pier and hurt my neck. The pain didn't go away, so a few weeks ago I had a scan done when we were docked in Florida. Make sure I hadn't busted anything, you know? The good news is my spine is fine, but the doctor spotted an abnormality in my neck. He wasn't a specialist, so he said he couldn't diagnose it, but he urged me to see someone. I did some research and that led me to Houston."

Shannon had reached over and taken his free hand in both of hers while he was talking. "*Abnormality?* What does that even mean?"

"There was a spot on the scan that shouldn't have been there."

"But that could be anything, right? People get weird benign growths all the time. *Benign.* That's the word, right? For the good kind of abnormality?"

He had been through the same thought spiral Shannon was currently in many times over the course of the last month. But right now he couldn't cling to the hope that it was nothing. He didn't want to hang his heart on likelihood or chance—he wanted truth. No matter what it was.

"The other day when I was gone? I was in Houston having a biopsy," he said. "They stuck this insanely tiny needle into my throat to remove cells and today they're supposed to tell me what's going on."

"But there's a chance it's not cancer?"

Wade sighed. "Let's just say, they didn't think the biopsy was going to shock them. And after everything I've read online, I'd be amazed if it was nothing."

"You're talking so robotically about this." She shook his hand. "Aren't you scared? I'm scared."

"They told me even if it's cancer that with this type, there doesn't have to be a huge hurry." He caught her gaze. "But, sis, I'm so freaked out. I just want it gone. Each time I look up thyroid cancer online, each time I read more, I get more freaked out. When I look in the mirror, all I can focus on is this lump in my throat."

Shannon reached over and ran her fingers lightly across his throat. "I don't feel anything."

Wade swallowed hard. When he touched his neck, the lump felt as if he had a golf ball stuck in there. It's all he felt.

"Let's work through this like the old days. Rational. Twin minds in sync." She took his hand again. "Just because they found it—if they even found anything—it could have been there for months, right? Even years. These things don't pop up overnight."

"True." He nodded. "That doesn't mean I want to sit on it now though." The fact was Wade was terrified. He hadn't gotten a full night's rest since the scan in Florida. Thoughts kept him up. Anxiety tapped cruel nails down his chest whenever he lay in bed. His throat would feel tight and he'd worry it was cancer growing. When he did sleep, his dreams turned sour—cancer taking over his body, cancer cells morphing outside his body and chasing him. It was easier not to sleep sometimes.

"Does Cassidy know?" Shannon's question pierced through his thoughts.

"No." His jaw tightened. "And I don't want her to."

"Wade."

"I'm serious, Shannon. Don't tell her."

"She has the right to know."

I don't think I can handle one more thing.

"What if I do find out it's a big nothing today? She would have worried needlessly. I won't do that to her." Cassidy might not care about him at all, but she would still worry if she knew because that's just the kind of person she was. She would worry because she had allowed Piper to meet him, and now what if he was suddenly gone again? She wouldn't want to deal with explaining why he disappeared if it was the worst-case scenario.

"Don't you think I've caused her enough grief in this life? I won't add to it, not if I can help it. Cassidy deserves less stress and hassle when it comes to me." She deserved so much more than Wade could have ever given her.

"What if this ends up being bad, Wade? What if we end up hearing what we don't want to?" Shannon asked quietly.

He lifted his hand away from hers to grip the steering wheel tighter than he needed to. He didn't want to think about possibly dying. Not now, when he was back home and slowly making strides with his family, when he had only just learned he had a daughter and Cassidy was back in his life.

Maybe the doctor would tell him it was nothing. Perhaps today would be the last appointment. The last sleepless night spent worrying.

"You have to tell her." Shannon broke through his thoughts.

Wade sighed. "Eventually I probably will."

Or possibly he would never have to burden her. That sounded better.

"Wade. Come on. This isn't something you keep to yourself."

"I'm not keeping it to myself, Shannon. You know."

"Only by seconds. You've been dealing with this a month, Wade. A month. And you haven't shared the load with anyone. That's not okay. It's not healthy, to say the least."

"Not true." He held up a finger. "I've shared it with God and that's enough."

"Is it?"

"Of course it is." His conversation with Cassidy that morning came back to mind. He had told her that God was a rescuer, someone she could run to for help. He couldn't spout out things like that and not believe them—not put them into action in his own life. God knew what he was facing; Wade prayed about it every day. Sometimes when the hard days came, Wade wondered if this was a punishment for all he had done wrong or a test to see if he would truly lean on God. Test if his faith was real. Wade got through those days by deciding he was going to withstand whatever this trial ended up being with God alone as his support. He would prove to God that he was a changed man too.

That's what faith was, wasn't it? Depending on God alone. That's what all the podcast preachers said.

Shannon shook her head. "But God put people in our lives to help us. We're supposed to trust others and live in community so we can share our loads. You can't read the depend-on-God parts of the Bible, only to ignore the love-one-another-and-take-care-of-each-other parts. Keeping this to yourself isn't the right thing to do."

"It is if you've already put everyone you care about through horrible trauma by faking your death, okay?" He was in a unique position, one where he had no right to rally troops to his side. Going through this virtually alone was a consequence of his horrible choices. One he would have to deal with. He had hurt and alienated his support system and he had no right to ask for their help. Not now, maybe not ever. "You're the only person I've told."

Shannon sucked in a breath. "You didn't tell Rhett?"

"Rhett's wedding is a month away. I want him to be able to be excited about that without anything tarnishing it. Especially me." He rolled his shoulders and switched to the slower lane of traffic. "So that's what I've been hiding. Now it's your turn."

Shannon set the bag of M&M's in the cup holder. They rattled together as the truck rolled down the highway.

She crossed her arms and looked out the passenger side window. "I'm not sure what you mean."

"Show me your arms." Wade jerked his chin toward her sweatshirt.

"What?"

"Don't play dumb." Wade had always been able to tell when Shannon was keeping something from him and likewise. They'd laughed about it when they were younger, calling it their twin minds. But Wade couldn't laugh now because he was almost certain of what she was hiding, and the thought of someone hurting his sister made his gut roil with a sick feeling. "The sweatshirt. You're covering bruises," he said quietly. "Am I wrong?"

She kept her gaze trained out the window. Her shoulders curved inward. "I want to leave him." Her voice was so small it was difficult to hear even though they didn't have the music on. "I've wanted to for a while." She finally turned toward Wade. A tear slipped down her cheek and it took everything inside of him not to jerk the truck to the side of the road and toss it into Park so he could hug his sister. That…or turn the truck around and hunt down Cord Anders. It was so tempting, but he knew getting his sister to talk about it would do more to end the situation than confronting Cord ever would.

Wade's friend Preach had left an abusive relationship at one point and they had talked at length about his past when they were stuck together for months working on the same yachts. Preach had said the thing that made him see the light was others seeing value in him, not people bad-talking the woman he had been in love with. The second the put-downs started, the victim wanted to defend the person, defend the choice they had made in being with that person.

Wade had witnessed Rhett confront Shannon about Cord a few times, asking her if Cord thought he was too good to come around the family, telling her Cord was controlling her. Each time, Shannon shrunk away from the family for the rest of the day. Wade didn't want that.

He needed to tread carefully. *God help me.*

Shannon needed to be encouraged and empowered, not condemned.

"How long has he been laying hands on you?"

"This has been the worst time." Shannon pushed up her sleeves, showing a patchwork map of purple, greenish and yellow-brown bruises. "I've started try-ing to stand up to him. Trying to leave him. But he gets so enraged when I tell him no or don't agree with him. The more I try, the more violent he's gotten."

Wade sucked in a sharp breath. He couldn't hold in his outburst. "He should be locked away for that." He needed to steady his anger. "Shannon, I love you and I would love to see you being treated with kindness and decency by a man who values all the things that are amazing about you. I would love to see a guy who trips over his own feet when he's around you because he's so into you he can't think straight. I love you and I'm really worried about you. I'm worried about what will happen if you're ever alone with him again."

"What if there isn't a guy like the one you described out there? What if no one ever sees me like that?"

He wanted to hug away her hurt so badly, but he knew that wouldn't make everything better like it had when they were kids. He wanted to tell her that plenty of good men would line up to date her if she was available, but empty promises wouldn't help. She needed sound reasoning. Wade glanced her way. "Better to be alone and know your value than have it dictated by how someone else treats you, don't you think? It can't feel good when he treats you like this."

"Of course it doesn't." She jerked down her sleeves. "But he was around. He was there when no one else was. Rhett and Macy are together and they're so perfect. Cassidy has Piper. Boone's got his family. Mom is… She's lost a lot of the time, Wade. I can't go to her. I can't count on her for companionship." Shannon pulled her knees up onto her seat and hugged them to her chest. "I don't want to be alone," she whispered. "I'm so tired of feeling like I've been left behind."

A thick feeling filled the back of Wade's throat and his eyes burned. Shannon had always been the most extroverted of the Jarrett siblings. She needed interaction, needed people in order to thrive. He put himself in her shoes over the last few years and it wasn't pretty. Alone, stressed with no one to lean on, desperate for anyone to be around. No wonder she had latched onto Cord when they had met. At first, his controlling ways had probably felt like care—as if someone cared enough to tell her what they thought about what she was doing. She had probably been frantic for any type of friendship, and once she had realized he wasn't the best choice for her, she had probably been in too deep and hadn't had anyone to go to for help.

If Wade had never left, could he have saved her from all the pain she was experiencing?

She wouldn't have been desperate for connection if he had stayed. If he had still been around to be her best friend. Yet another consequence of his selfish choices.

A sharp pain went through his chest.

"You won't be alone. I'm here, Shannon. You don't have to be alone anymore." He would help her break free of Cord. He would do whatever he had to in order for her to be safe and thriving again.

"You're here for treatment, Wade. Not for us."

After all they had discussed, her accusatory tone took him by surprise. Her words stung.

"What?"

"You said yourself that after the doctor found the abnormality, you researched and Houston had good doctors. That's what brought you home," she said. "Not us. Not a desire to make things right with your family."

"That's not fair."

"If you didn't have a medical issue, would you have come back? Be honest."

He wanted to say that the articles about a tornado destroying Red Dog Ranch would have been enough. And certainly stumbling upon his father's obituary had been a huge wake-up call. But would he have returned or would he have read those things and figured they were better off without him? He'd had the thought enough times to know the truth.

Everyone was better off without him.

It had been his mantra for so long, it was hard to shake. But the conversation with Shannon proved that wasn't exactly true.

"I don't know," he muttered.

"Well, I do. You're here for you. Not for us."

"The cancer scare might have been what brought me here." He glanced her way, catching her eye for a second before looking back at the highway. "But it's not why I'm going to stay. I'm staying because I love you guys and I was an idiot for so many years and I'm never walking away from the people I love again."

Silence stretched between them for ten miles of road. Wade was afraid it might stay that way until they reached Houston.

Shannon finally broke it. "Wade?"

"Hmm?"

"I'm scared. Of Cord. Of leaving. Of what will happen."

Wade reached across the divide and took her hand. "When we get back to town, would you be willing to go to the police department? You need to file a report.

There needs to be a record of Cord's behavior and then, if you are willing, we can call Cord and you can tell him it's over." He wanted her to take action while her mind was set against Cord. Abusers were so good at manipulating their victims, he didn't want Cord to have a chance to mess with her emotions ever again. "I'll stay with you the whole time. Every step of this."

"I'll do it. File a report." She nodded. "I'm ready. Honestly, I think I've been ready since the tornado." She hugged her stomach. "I feel so stupid that I've let this go on for so long. How did I let this happen?"

"Don't judge yourself in this moment."

"It feels impossible not to."

Wade tapped the steering wheel. "Today isn't the finish line to who you will become. Okay?"

Her smile was timid. "For you either."

He rubbed the heel of his hand against his chest, emotions and thoughts pulling it tight.

He would never leave his family again.

Chapter Seven

Cassidy heaved her backpack onto her kitchen counter and shoved a travel pack of wet wipes, two more small bags of Goldfish crackers and a tube of antiseptic cream inside. Most of the ranch staff, Cassidy and Piper included, had eaten a light supper of chipotle honey chicken skewers at the dining hall an hour ago but snacks were always a good idea.

Wade and Shannon hadn't been at dinner. It was the second night in a row they had missed it after saying they might be there. First, the tacos last night to celebrate Piper's cast-free status and then tonight. Should she text Wade—ask if he needed something to eat before they headed out? Cassidy pushed that thought away. Wade was a grown man who could take care of himself. He hardly needed her fussing over him. If he hadn't eaten something before hiking, that was his problem.

With a growl, she tucked three protein bars into the bag not ten seconds later. They were the mint-chocolate-flavored bars, which she had learned a few days ago were his favorites. Simply so he didn't pass out. She couldn't exactly carry him if something happened. That's the only reason she was letting those things take up space in her pack.

Maybe if she repeated it quickly three times, it would be true.

"Sunblock," she mumbled and took off toward the bathroom to find a fresh tube. She came back with sunblock, lip balm, more Band-Aids and a hairbrush. "Who goes hiking in the heat of summer? Honestly."

"I do, Mom! We're going to have so much fun. I love to hike. Don't I?" Piper danced around in the living room with a purple ribbon in her hand. Cloudstorm trailed her, pouncing and nipping at the end of the ribbon.

"You'll love it, sweetheart."

Cassidy halted her preparations to take in her daughter's joy. Why had she held off on giving her a cat for so long? The responsibility was helping Piper thrive. Piper had started waking up earlier than normal to feed the cat and give him fresh water. She patiently brushed him every day and kept her room straight because she said Cloudstorm liked it better that way. She snuggled with him and talked to the cat as if he was a best friend.

Cassidy still stood by what she had told Wade—he couldn't buy Piper's love or favor. A beloved pet wouldn't erase five years of his not being there. But having Cloudstorm wasn't too bad. Especially when he curled up on Cassidy's lap on the couch each night after she put Piper to bed, purring like a tiny lawn mower. A content little ball of fluff warming her during the time of day when loneliness usually struck the hardest.

Deep down Cassidy knew she would have probably

never let Piper have a cat. Because pets had a special way of winding themselves around a person's heart, but they didn't live as long as their humans did. Loving a pet almost guaranteed a very hard goodbye down the road. It had been silly and cowardly. Piper had Sheep, after all. But ponies were known to live into their thirties if not forties. More than likely Piper would be grown by the time she had to say goodbye to her beloved little horse so that hadn't triggered Cassidy as much as the thought of a cat had.

Selfishly, Cassidy hadn't wanted to let another living being into her house, into her heart, only to go through losing them. Even a small cat. She had faced too many losses in her life. First Wade, then her parents kicking her out of their lives, Mrs. Jarrett starting to fade and Mr. Jarrett's sudden passing had hit them all hard. There was also Rhett, who had left the ranch without saying a word a few years ago and Boone and his family had moved away last year. Cassidy knew she couldn't keep people or relationships the same forever— people grew and changed. But it seemed like everyone moved on from her so easily. No one besides Piper truly needed her or stuck around for her. The Jarretts were the only family she had and all of them seemed to be slipping away.

How are my two favorite ladies?

Wade had included her in that statement. Cassidy Danvers. The girl who was so easy to walk away from. But he had always had a way with words. She couldn't put too much stock in little things he said in passing.

"Will Daddy be here soon?" Piper scooped Cloudstorm up like a baby.

Cassidy checked her watch. If he had forgotten about them, he would get an earful from her.

He better keep his word to Piper.

"Soon, baby."

Thinking of him made her pulse kick up. Cassidy wasn't certain if it was because she was frustrated with his missing dinner last night after Piper had been looking forward to seeing him. Or perhaps it was the memory of his hand on her leg in the car and the way he looked at her as if whatever Cassidy was saying was the most important thing happening on the planet in that moment.

The night last week outside her home when she had wanted to kiss him rushed to the forefront of her mind.

Both reasons.

She was frustrated with him for getting their daughter's hopes up and frustrated with herself for still being affected by him.

When her doorbell rang, Cassidy pawed through the bag for the third time, checking to make sure she had full changes of clothes for both Piper and herself. Piper bounded to open the door and flung herself into Wade's arms. He spun her around once and then dropped a kiss to the top of her head.

"Good to see you, buddy."

Piper flexed her arm to show off a muscle. "Look."

"Wow. That arm is looking strong already." He moved her to his hip and crossed the room to where Cassidy was rearranging her bag. "Is it okay with you guys if Aunt Shannon joins us tonight? She really wants to see the sunset at Enchanted Rock. We haven't been there since we were kids."

"I've never been," Piper said loudly. "Not ever."

"Well, you won't be able to say that for much longer," Wade said.

Cassidy relaxed her shoulders. Having Shannon with them eased any awkwardness there might have been with the three of them going out as a family. She snapped empty water bottles to the sides of her bag. They would fill them at the fountain when they got there instead of risk them spilling in the car. "We'd love to have Shannon along, wouldn't we, Piper?"

Piper had her arms looped around Wade's neck. "Fine with me."

Wade winked at her. "Good, because she's in the car waiting for you." Piper wiggled out of his arms and raced outside.

"Here." Wade reached for the backpack. "I can carry that." He heaved it onto his back with an exaggerated groan and pretended to stumble a little under the weight. "What did you pack in here? My guess is bricks. You're planning to build a house at the top, aren't you?"

Cassidy rolled her eyes. "Stuff we need."

Wade's left eyebrow rose and the ever-present quirk in his mouth looked close to breaking into a smile. "The trail to the top is only a half mile."

"Up a ridiculously steep incline, if I remember correctly. Some of it's near vertical." Cassidy shoved a hair tie onto her wrist and then another one in case Shannon needed one or if she lost the first one on the climb. Her daughter's hair was already tightly bound in her usual double braids. "Piper is almost five and she's got a lot of energy, but you better be ready to lug her at least half the way up and most of the way down."

"Almost five," he repeated softly. His near-smile completely fell away from his handsome face, making him look so downcast, so lost. "I don't even know when her birthday is. I can't believe I haven't asked that yet."

Every cell in Cassidy's body wanted to reach out and comfort him. Touch her fingertips to his cheek and wipe away his hurt. It wasn't his fault, not this. Still, her desire to reach out to him made no sense. She shoved her hands into her pockets.

"Two weeks from tomorrow."

Wade nodded. "I'll be there."

"Will you?"

"Cass, we have got to—"

Cassidy's voice trembled as she barreled ahead. "Because she stood by the doors of the dining hall for most of supper last night watching for you and you never came. Today she looked for you all day and you weren't around. We can't do this each time. I won't let her spend her life waiting for you."

Like Cassidy had.

Wade grabbed hold of the backpack's straps, the muscles in his arms bunching. "I said I'd try. I didn't say I'd for sure be there. If I had promised to be there, nothing would have kept me away. I don't understand why this is such a big issue."

"She's young, Wade. She can't mince through meanings like that yet. To her, *try* means you'll do everything you can to be there." Cassidy pressed a hand to her temple. "It's stuff like this that worries me. You not following through. Her little heart strung along."

His mouth opened, closed, then, "That's not fair. I'm

guilty of a lot in my life but not following through with Piper isn't one of them and I don't plan for it to ever be."

"Where were you?" She knew she had no right to ask, but she asked anyway. Wade was keeping something from her. That much was clear.

"I was doing something really important."

"Your *child* is really important." Cassidy jammed a finger against the top of the counter a few times as she made her point.

"I know, Cassidy." Wade threw his hands up. "Believe me, I know that. You guys are the most important people in my world but I care about my family too." He swept a hand in the direction of the big Jarrett house. "So if one of them needs help, I'm going to help them. Especially if I can do so without breaking my word to you or our daughter, which is what I was doing when I skipped dinner yesterday. Today too, actually."

Cassidy's irritation flashed away as quickly as it had come. One of the Jarretts needed help? Why didn't she know?

"Who?"

He shook his head. "It's not for me to tell."

Seriously? He wasn't going to tell her. For the last five years, she had only stood by his family and pitched in at the ranch in every way imaginable to help the Jarretts. Cassidy had grown far closer to them than she had ever been with her own parents. Wade hadn't been there for them. Wade had hurt them. But they trusted him—involved him—already.

And now they were keeping things from her.

Cassidy's hands trembled. She straightened some

paperwork on the counter to keep them busy. To keep Wade from noticing.

Their beloved Wade had returned and apparently that meant she could be iced out. Why bother with the ex-girlfriend when they had him?

Fear chased hurt through her head, down her spine. They churned into something ugly in her stomach.

She crossed her arms in an attempt to shield herself from the effect Wade had on her. "Were *you* the one who needed help? You haven't been back two whole weeks but you've disappeared three full days. Where are you going?" Cassidy stepped closer. She lifted her chin. "If you are gambling again... I can't, Wade. You can't be a part of our lives if you've fallen into any of that stuff again."

"Whoa." He held up both hands and took a step back, creating space. "A little faith here." He turned away from her, dug his hands into his hair and tugged on the strands. When he turned back to her, his hair was completely disheveled and charmingly distracting.

She tightened her crossed arms. *Focus, Cassidy.*

"Am I acting like I'm drunk or being chased down by goons for gaming debts?" He pressed a palm to his chest. "Come on, Cassidy. I'm working myself ragged out there and spending all my time with you guys and my family." He held up a finger, stemming her words. "And I love it. I don't want to be spending my time doing anything else. But it's highly irritating to be constantly doubted after all that."

"Mom. Dad." Piper burst through the front door. "Shannon says we have to get a move on." She ran back to the car, leaving the front door to Cassidy's bungalow wide open.

Cassidy moved to follow her but Wade sidestepped, getting in her way. "We need to settle this before we head out. Do you honestly believe I'm still involved in those things?" he asked in a voice so raw a tsunami of regret flooded through her.

She met his leaf-green gaze. His eyes were bright and no worry creased his features.

"You're clean," she conceded. "By the looks of it, you've been clean for a long time." She sighed. "I shouldn't have said what I did. It just…came out."

He nodded, once, tightly.

"Wade." She caught his arm when he made a move to leave. "I'm sorry. Forgive me for saying that."

Half the reason she had snapped at him was because she had missed him at supper the day Piper had her cast removed. And Cassidy had missed him most of today when she had found out he wasn't at the ranch. *She* was beginning to seek out his face, expect his smile and listen for his tender words. He hadn't been home long and yet Wade had already taken back the part of her heart that had always been his.

All of it.

Which terrified her. She couldn't lose herself to Wade Jarrett again. Not without knowing he was going to put down roots at Red Dog Ranch for good. She couldn't go through loving and losing him again. She wouldn't.

He blew out a long stream of air as he shoved a hand through his hair. "It's fine. I don't have a good track record so it shouldn't bother me so much when you think the worst."

"But it does bother you."

"I wish it wasn't the initial conclusion jumped to. But what can I do?" He shrugged.

"I shouldn't have said it."

"I'm not that guy anymore, Cass. I don't know how to make you believe that and maybe I just need to come to terms with the fact that people will always think the worst about me. But I'd like to change opinions if I can." His gaze latched onto hers. "I'd do anything to change your opinion."

"You are," she whispered. "Every day. You are."

Wade looked around her house, glancing toward the open front door. "If we don't head out soon Shannon and Piper might take off without us." He held out his hand. "Truce?"

She surprised herself by taking it.

And was even more surprised to find she didn't want to let go.

As Wade inched the car out onto the road, he was sure everyone in it could hear his heart pounding. See the beads of sweat skating down his back.

That had been way too close. He'd almost told Cassidy. Almost blurted everything out when she was grilling him.

Oh, by the way, I have cancer, Cassidy.

That would have gone over great.

At the medical center yesterday, Wade's doctor had confirmed his fears. Papillary carcinoma, he had called it. The most common kind of thyroid cancer—

information that was supposed to be reassuring but shockingly hadn't helped Wade sleep any better. The doctor had explained to him that it was usually a slow-growing kind, so he had mused that Wade must have had it for a while. There was a risk of this type of cancer moving into the lymph nodes though, so he had been urged to schedule the surgery right away. The team of specialists needed to get in there and remove anything that looked incorrect.

In eleven days, he would have a lobectomy.

Wade fought the urge to touch his neck.

If all went well, in eleven days, all the cancer would be removed from his body and he could move on. If healing went according to the doctor's plans, he would never have to worry anyone besides Shannon. He would be able to attend Rhett's wedding without anyone being the wiser.

Okay, the doctor explained he would have a scar and that the scar would be fairly visible in the beginning and then fade over time. But he hoped a good tie or high-collared shirt would be able to hide it. He would figure out something.

And if he ended up having to tell them, by then it would be behind him and something they could celebrate instead of worry about.

If all went according to plan.

All that mattered was Wade would be able to spare Cassidy any worry she would have had if she had known his diagnosis. By dealing with this on his own as much as he could, he wouldn't be a burden to anyone. He had caused them all enough grief five years ago and any opportunity to save them from more he'd take. Especially for Cassidy, who had already admitted to being wrung out about his being back. She was starting to talk to him and he didn't want to give her cause to pull away.

In the passenger seat, Cassidy fished a tube of lip balm out of the backpack she had insisted on stowing on her floorboard and handed it to Piper. Wade's mouth went dry. Cassidy was the kindest, best person he had ever met. She thought of everyone's needs and made sure everyone knew how much she cared about them in so many little ways. She had always made him want to be a better man. To live up to the person she believed he could be.

He loved her. He had never stopped loving Cassidy Danvers and he never would.

Acknowledging that didn't change the fact that Cassidy could do a million times better than the guy who had let her down when she had needed him the most. It didn't change the fact that he was a total mess and still needed to focus on fixing his relationships with his family.

Shannon was warming up to him. She had trusted him enough to let him come with her to file for a protective order at the courthouse today. Last night after the cops had photographed Shannon's bruises, they had arrested Cord on a domestic assault charge but he had bonded out quickly this morning before they had been able to get the protective order approved. However, the people at the courthouse had assured them he would be served with notice soon, not that a piece of paper would keep a man like Cord away, but at least they could call the cops if he did show up and there would be enforceable action beyond them just asking him to stay away.

They would have to tell the rest of the family soon, but Shannon had made him promise to allow her to be the one to say something.

As far as Wade's family went, Rhett would take more time. And Boone hadn't returned any of his calls, although Shannon assured Wade that Boone was really busy between studying for his classes at divinity school and his family. They had exchanged a couple emails where Boone wrote that Wade was forgiven, but Wade would have actually liked to talk to him before checking off their relationship as on the right track again.

Shannon hooked her arm on the edge of his seat and leaned forward to speak with him and Cassidy. "I hope these clouds clear out before sunset." She pointed at the gray puffs obscuring the sun. "After waiting in line for the vouchers this morning, I'd be disappointed if we don't get a great sunset."

Enchanted Rock was a large granite dome that looked like an Easter egg lying on its side in the middle of Texas. A popular tourist attraction in the area, the park often reached capacity by ten in the morning. At that point, they handed out vouchers for people to return later in the day. Shannon and Wade had waited in a ninety-minute line that morning to get their return voucher, but that had been Wade's plan all along. Growing up, his father had taken the family hiking all over Texas but Wade had the best memories of watching sunsets from the top of Enchanted Rock. He had wanted Piper and Cassidy to witness it too.

"We'll still have fun, even if we don't get to see a sunset," Cassidy said.

Piper tapped on the window. "Maybe it'll storm *real* bad."

Wade chuckled over Piper's delivery. "It's not supposed to rain at all. I checked the weather earlier. They said there's a zero percent chance."

"But," Piper dragged out the word. "Even if there was, storms are okay."

"You're right," Cassidy said. "We don't need to be afraid of storms. It's just not very fun to be stuck in one outside. Especially on granite because it gets really slippery."

"Remember the tornado?" Piper whispered.

Cassidy's caught Wade's eyes. Her brow creased.

In the spring, a tornado had torn a path through Red Dog Ranch and Piper had been on the property when it happened. He had heard how Cassidy and Piper had huddled in the basement of the dining hall with a bunch of guests who had come for an Easter event at the ranch. Tightness corded around Wade's chest. His sweet daughter had been in danger and he hadn't been there to help her or hold her or keep her safe.

Cassidy's gaze was pleading.

He hadn't been able to help her then, but he could step in and be there for Piper now.

Wade rolled his shoulders. "You don't have to worry, sweetheart. There aren't any tornadoes in the forecast. These clouds should be out of our way soon. I wouldn't take you out if I hadn't checked to make sure it was safe first."

"Listen to me." Piper's little voice was firm. "I'm not worried. I have to tell you something."

Cassidy twisted in her chair. "What did you want to tell us? Go ahead, Piper."

"Uncle Rhett told me he knew he loved Macy because of the tornado. So that's not bad. What if the storm hadn't come? He still wouldn't know."

Shannon set her hand on Piper's arm. "He would have figured it out eventually. Rhett is stubborn, but I have confidence he would have realized he loved Macy without a storm."

Piper jerked her head back and forth, braids flying. "The storm made Uncle Rhett like the ranch too. Before, he didn't. Remember?" Her voice rose. She pointed at Shannon. "And ever since the storm, you've been home more too. I like that. So that's a good thing. I think the storm made a lot of good things happen."

Shannon swiped at her eyes. "Thanks, sweet lady. I'm glad I'm home more too."

"But the big thing." Piper held up her arms, fingers splayed. "The really big, really important thing is that the storm brought my dad home."

Cassidy's hand immediately snaked out to clasp one of his.

Before, Wade had been a disappointment to his family; he didn't know how to take being considered someone's blessing.

Wade swallowed, coughed, cleared his throat. "I love you so much. You know that, don't you, Piper?"

"I know, Daddy. To the moon."

"And back," Wade said. In a quick motion, Wade flipped his hand over so he could lace his fingers with Cassidy's. She didn't pull away.

His daughter nodded. "People think storms are the

bad guys. But know what? A lot of bad things happened like the cabins and the office and all those cars flipped over *but* the tornado made our lives better. I mean, after the storm. Like, bigger parts of our lives than all the stuff, right?"

"You're right, Piper. That's all really good to remember. I don't think I had made those connections," Cassidy said.

"That's why I named my cat Cloudstorm. So I can remember about the storms." She tapped her forehead. "Maybe they are scary, but I have to be brave because they can be good after they're done."

"I thought you named him that because he's gray and white like clouds?" Shannon's smile said she was teasing.

Piper shrugged. "Well, that too." Her eyes zeroed in on Wade. "I'm glad you're back, Dad."

"I'm glad too."

Wade pulled into the Enchanted Rock parking lot. The pink dome of the rock formation loomed ahead of them.

"How come you left?" Piper's brow scrunched up. "Where were you?"

Wade had known these questions would come at some point. He had been prepared to explain his actions to Cassidy but telling Piper was a different matter. She was so young—would she understand? He needed to speak in terms she could grasp. At least, he hoped he could.

Cassidy squeezed his hand. "Right now's probably not the best time, Piper."

He found a parking spot, parked the car but left the

keys in so the air could run. He unbuckled his seat belt and turned so he could look at Piper.

"It's fine." Wade rubbed his hand over the back of his neck. "I—ah—I wasn't a good person, when I was younger."

"Like how I'm young?" Piper pointed at herself.

"No, I was older than you. When I was a teenager. Do you know what a teenager is?"

"Yeah, Dad." She rolled her eyes. He wasn't aware almost-five-year-olds knew to roll their eyes, but apparently they did. "A big kid."

"Right." He nodded. "When I was a big kid, I wasn't a good person."

"Mommy liked you." Piper looked to Cassidy. "She said you were the best. She told me that all the time."

Don't glance at Cassidy.

Don't glance at Cassidy.

He didn't want to make things awkward for either of them, so he kept his gaze squarely on Piper. "Well, your mommy had a way of seeing who I could be and she cared about that person."

"False." Cassidy's whisper was hoarse. Wade looked her way to find she was looking right at him. "I cared about your daddy as-is. That means, I didn't ask him or expect him to be anyone else. He did do bad things, but that doesn't make someone bad. It means they made mistakes, and haven't we all?" She finally broke eye contact to address their daughter. "Do you understand?"

"Like when I broke your favorite vase and hid it under the sink." Piper's shoulders dropped as she trained her attention on her hands. "I wasn't a bad person. But it was a bad thing to do."

"Exactly."

"What bad thing did you do, Dad?"

How did he explain underage drinking and gambling to a little kid? How did he explain addiction and what it could turn a person into, even when they were trying to fight it? Piper couldn't comprehend how years' worth of feeling as if he didn't measure up to his siblings could be forgotten as long as he had tossed himself fully into one of his preferred vices. He prayed she would never have cause to understand the paths he had walked and what he had forfeited in the name of the next high.

Wade shifted in his seat. Despite the air-conditioning blasting through the cabin, he felt hot. He tugged at his shirt collar. "I was doing things I shouldn't have been doing and not living in a way that made God happy. God wasn't my friend yet back then. A lot of my choices made my family sad. They made your mom sad too."

Cassidy opened her mouth to interject, but Wade shook his head.

"Some friends and I were going on a trip. I had always planned to come home, but then there was a storm on the water and our ship went down." He wanted to make sure Cassidy and Shannon heard he hadn't kissed them goodbye on his way out the door with the knowledge he wasn't going to return. Nothing had been premeditated. He thought that was important for them to know.

"Some other people with a boat saved me. When I saw all my friends had died… I just… I thought I deserved to be with them. I thought about your mom and my family and it hit me that their lives might be better if I weren't around to disappoint them anymore." Wade swallowed hard. "I wanted your mom to be happy and I knew she never could be with me. So I stayed away and I let people think whatever they wanted."

"So it wasn't—wasn't because you didn't love us?" Piper's voice quivered.

Her tears tore at his heart in a way that made him feel split in two. He reached over the seats, fumbling to get her unclipped from her car seat. Shannon swooped her hands under his and deftly unbuckled Piper. Then Wade took Piper in his arms and hauled her onto his lap in the front seat. He hugged her close.

He could have reminded her he hadn't known about her. He could have absolved himself of her pain and pushed it onto Cassidy. But he wouldn't. Piper was in pain and he would do whatever he could to make it go away, and casting her mother in a bad light wouldn't do that. Five years ago, Cassidy had good reason not to trust he would change his life to be a good father. He didn't blame her for not telling.

"Piper, sweetheart." He stroked her hair, her back. "Your mom was the most important person in my life and I loved everyone at Red Dog Ranch so, so much. Because I loved them, it hurt to know that I kept making them sad. I didn't want them to ever be sad again. I stayed away *because* I loved them." He tucked her head under his chin and kept his arms around her until her tears stopped.

After a few minutes, Piper sat up, took a deep rattling breath and wiped at her face. "Well, we're here. What are we waiting for?"

Shannon, Wade and Cassidy all started laughing.

"Oh, to be young and resilient." Shannon flung open her car door and clambered out.

Wade helped Piper out of the front seat, then he slung Cassidy's pack over his shoulders. Shannon wore a small backpack that was really a water bottle. Wade locked up the car and stared toward Enchanted Rock. It looked as steep as he remembered, but he was pretty sure he had faced a bigger mountain already today.

Chapter Eight

Enchanted Rock sprang up ahead of them. A giant pink rock surrounded by rubble, trails and a cactus forest. Even though Cassidy had made the trek to the top before with no issues, today it looked a bit daunting.

She came alongside Piper when they started on the path marked Summit Trail. "You sure you're up for this? Because it's okay if you're not."

Piper was at an age where her emotions could be consuming. Her tears in the car during the talk with Wade had twisted Cassidy's heart. She very well could have been exhausted from processing everything. In the past, she had explained to Piper that before he died, her dad hadn't known she was going to be born. But Piper might not have understood what that meant. Or maybe she had wondered if that had been made-up the same as her dad's passing.

Piper blew her bangs out of her eyes. "I'm fine, Mom."

"It's just we're already up way past your bedtime and I know I said that would be fine for a special event, but if it's too much you say so, okay? It's fine if we have to turn around or do this another time. Right, everyone?"

Wade and Shannon were near the water fountain filling up all their water bottles. They both chimed in with their agreement.

"Or if you need to stop for a rest. Just speak up," Wade added.

"I won't need to stop. Shannon and I will beat you to the top because we're younger than you!" Piper skipped ahead on the path, grabbing Shannon's hand along the way.

Shannon looked back over her shoulder. "So I guess that's game on, then."

Wade laughed. "I call foul. Shannon's only younger than me by two minutes!"

"And hello," Cassidy said. "I'm a whole year younger than the twins. Which makes me the second youngest here. Thank you very much."

"Hang on." Wade motioned for Shannon and Piper to wait. "We all want to have fun but some safety things before we have people rushing off. That rock—" he pointed at Enchanted Rock "—is 425 feet high and it's steep most of the way up. So pace yourselves and drink lots of water along the way."

"Got it." Shannon saluted him.

Cassidy couldn't help the grin that appeared on her face. Wade was home. Wade and Shannon were acting like *The Twins* again. And despite the heated words they had exchanged back at Cassidy's house, Wade was trying to be a present and involved father. That was a lot given the fact that only a few weeks ago he hadn't even known he was one.

"Not finished yet." Wade's mouth quirked with one of his almost-smiles. "When you hit the slope, it'll go better for you if you zigzag as you walk. Remember, we still have to climb back down so don't use all your energy to get to the top." He had caught up to them and was leaning over like a football coach rattling off game-winning plays. "The snakes love this area so keep your eyes peeled for rattlers and copperheads—especially the copperheads—they can blend right in to the surrounding here. And avoid Turkey Peak." He pointed in the direction of an outcropping of rocks. "I know it looks tempting, but it's a sheer rock face climb up a dense cactus forest. We're just doing the big rock today. Nothing else. Any questions?"

"Yeah, I've got a question." Shannon raised her hand. "Since when did you become a park ranger?"

"I'll tell you when Cass and I beat you to the top."

"So not happening," Shannon said as she and Piper set off at a brisk pace. Piper spun around and stuck her tongue out at them before jogging to catch up with Shannon again.

Cassidy tugged on her lower lip as she watched them charge ahead. "Maybe we should all stay together." She started after them.

Wade kept pace beside her. "They'll be fine. Let them have fun. I think they both need it."

"Didn't Shannon lose her phone or something? What if something happens?"

Wade adjusted the straps on the backpack, shifting its weight a little. She had packed way too much stuff in there and it had to weigh a ton now that it had two full water bottles attached as well.

"I got her one of those phones you buy with minutes loaded on them," Wade said. "I have her number, she has mine. If they need to reach us, they'll be able to." Then gently, "Shannon won't let anything happen to Piper."

Their shoes crunched along the path in sync. Cassidy caught Wade glancing her way every few seconds. Warmth crept across the back of her neck and her cheeks, and she wondered if it was the heat rolling off the sunbaked earth that was causing her flush or remembering how she and Wade had held hands in the car.

Was it juvenile to get a thrill from something as small as hand-holding? Maybe. But Cassidy had dated Wade when they were both teens and she hadn't done much dating since. Hand-holding still meant something to her. Honestly, she hoped it would always be a big deal. If she ever got married, she wanted to be one of those couples holding hands while they shuffled through the grocery store together when they were in their eighties.

She still wasn't sure she could walk down a romantic road with Wade again. Her heart might never be ready to trust like that, but she was enjoying spending time with him and that could only help with them co-parenting and living on the same swath of land.

She would be careful. She would not get in over her head.

A small voice inside told her she already was, but she batted it away.

Wade cleared his throat. "Everything Piper said in the car. About the storms. She's so smart." He grinned her way. "Are you sure she's really mine, because I'm not at all—"

Cassidy swatted his shoulder.

"You were always smart. Probably too smart for your own good," she said. "You just didn't feel the need to apply yourself in school."

"You're not wrong about the school part."

Cassidy bumped her shoulder into Wade's. "She was right, you know. About the tornado bringing good things. Bigger than that too. That good can come out of things we think would destroy us." She sucked in a humid breath before plunging onward. "I didn't know you felt that way—that you thought you were holding me back from happiness."

He hiked one shoulder. "You wouldn't let me tell you when I tried."

Your mom was the most important person in my life. I wanted your mom to be happy and I knew she never could be with me.

She touched his elbow. "You were wrong though."

"I find I usually am." He glanced her way, wearing a timid smile that sent her pulse into danger zones.

That vulnerable smile unglued her lips, setting free unguarded words. "I never found happiness again. Not without you. That wouldn't have been possible."

"Cassidy." He sucked in a sharp breath. "Tell me you're not still thinking of moving into town. I didn't bring it up before…but now…I need to know."

It had only been a week or so ago, but it felt like forever. So much had changed so quickly.

Cassidy barked out a laugh. "Definitely not. I feel bad for the realtor. I think he thought I would be an easy sell, but once I got back to the ranch, I knew I couldn't leave. I looked myself in the mirror and decided I would be strong enough to figure out how to navigate my life with you sharing the ranch."

"And are you? Strong enough, I mean?" He winced. "That came out wrong. All I mean is if you need me to give you space or if there's something I can do to make this transition less uncomfortable for you, just say the word. I'll do anything for you guys."

She studied his profile bathed in the light of the evening sun and the world fell away. There wasn't a climb in front of her. There weren't things to do at home. There was only Wade, gorgeous and kind and hard-working and compassionate Wade.

Was she strong enough to be around Wade and not fall for him?

Probably not.

She shook her head. He didn't need to change anything.

They hiked for a few minutes, pointing out interesting rock formations to each other and stopping once to both guzzle water and take a quick selfie with Enchanted Rock in the background. When they came to an area that was strewn with different sized boulders, Wade took her hand and helped her cross back to the solid rock face. The path narrowed so with each step they were brushing hips and elbows. There were plenty of people all over the state park but on this part of the path, it felt as if they were the only ones.

It felt safe.

"Going back to what we were talking about before," she said. "Since realizing you were alive, I kept thinking that you rejected me. You wanted to leave me and didn't want to deal with the breakup. It was hard to reconcile that with how we were when we were together." They had been one of those couples who only saw each other and tried to spend as much time as they could together. Wade had always seemed happy—more than that. He had been completely enamored with Cassidy. So the idea that he had faked that feeling over the years they dated had really thrown her for a loop. She had questioned if she could ever trust someone else's love.

Wade came to a stop. She had to halt and turn to face him.

His eyes latched onto hers. He whispered, "Because it wasn't true."

Cassidy's hands shook. "I know that now."

"That first day back I said I loved you." He inched closer until they were standing breaths away. "I said I left for you. I wanted what was best for you and that wasn't ever going to be me."

She ducked her head. "I get that now. And for the record, I think you were so incredibly wrong to do that. You had no right to make that choice for us, for me, without involving me. But I'm beginning to see that what I thought was rejection was actually my rescue."

His left eyebrow went up. "Yeah?"

She started walking again and he fell into step beside her.

"When we thought you were dead—after we accepted it and had a funeral—I was very lost, Wade." He had been her life to a very unhealthy extent when they were dating. It was hard to figure out life with the axis of her world suddenly gone. "And when I was lost, I finally broke down and went to God for the first time." She laughed softly. "I mean, it was almost impossible not to end up at church living with your family. But it was good. Very hard, but good because that's what led me to become a Christian. Would I be one if we had been together all this time? I'd like to think so, but I don't know."

"I'm glad you found God, Cassidy. After I did, I prayed for you all the time. Every single day."

In the car, he had been so vulnerable and honest answering Piper's questions. Watching them interact while he handled a hard talk had softened Cassidy's heart toward him completely. Hearing he had been praying for her this whole time? Cassidy had to blink back tears.

"You know," she admitted. "I've been angry with God since you came back."

"Angry He let me live?"

She grabbed his bicep and jiggled on his arm. "Don't even joke about that." She let go just as quickly, keeping up their brisk pace. "Angry because I had cried out to God again and again about you. I begged for you to turn up somewhere. I wept to Him and that whole time He knew you were alive. It felt as if you had both played this big trick on me. I felt betrayed."

Wade looked out over the distance for the space of a few heartbeats. "I think sometimes God has to let our hearts break or else we would never be ready to acknowledge we need Him to save us. When you look back at every story in the Bible, pain has always been a part of the process. Trying to outrun the hard times ends up costing us more than submission ever will. I'm afraid my life is an example of that. The how-not-to example."

He still thought he was a failure. A mess-up.

She wanted to hug him until all the lies he believed about himself faded away.

Wade was an overcomer. He was a passionate, dedicated man who was committed to walking a straight path in life.

If only he could see himself through her eyes.

"I don't know. You seem to have turned out just— Ooh, ouch!" Cassidy's boot caught on a rock and she lost her balance. Landing on her hands and knees, the momentum skidded her forward over a patch of sharp pebbles.

Wade tromped after her. One of his arms looped around her and the other slipped under her knees and she was up, cradled against his chest a second later.

He scanned her face. "What hurts?"

His heart pounded against her side as she was enveloped in his ocean-and-midnight scent. There was some sweat there too, which only made him more appealing. It was enough to make Cassidy forget he had asked her a question.

Wade's brow dipped. "Did you hit your head?"

She shook herself out of the schoolgirl-crush tunnel vision Wade's proximity was known to bring on. "I'm fine. Scrapes." She held up a bloody palm. "Nothing major. I can walk." She pressed a hand to his chest.

Wade tightened his hold. "These large rocks look like snake haven. Let me get you someplace better." He started gingerly over the area where she had slipped. His breath was slightly labored, which was to be expected when he was carrying her and a backpack on an incline in the middle of summer in Texas. He set her down away from the strewn path on a rock that was about the height of a chair.

He slung the backpack off and unzipped the top. "Tell me you packed some first aid supplies along with the heavy gold bricks." He located the antiseptic cream, wet wipes and a hoard of bandages and set them beside her. Her hands were a little torn up and the knee on her right pant leg was ripped open and bloody. Wade unscrewed one of the water bottles and poured water over both her hands, then he had her rest her leg on top of another rock so he could pull a few rock shards out of her knee and pour water over that wound too. He dabbed each area with wet wipes. "I don't know if these are the best, but they're all we have." And then he applied the first aid cream and bandages to the worst parts. Mostly on her knee and one deeper cut in her palm.

When he was studying her knee, she reflexively reached forward and brushed some of his hair away from his forehead. Wade leaned into the touch.

"Hey, Wade?" She knew if she slipped her hand to the back of his head, if she tipped her head toward his, he would kiss her. Every cell in Cassidy's body knew it. She let her hand drop to her side. "I'm glad you're alive."

He got to his feet, grinned down at her and offered his hand. "You have mentioned that once or twice. But it's nice to be reminded."

She licked her lips. Took his hand and got to her feet. "If we could go back… If you could have a do-over, would you?"

"I want to say yes, but I mean, it's complicated. We wouldn't have turned out like we both are now. What we each faced formed us into who we are." He sighed.

"I guess what I'm saying is I don't think wishing for do-overs is healthy for anyone at this point. Would I like to have spared everyone the anguish I caused? Absolutely. But would I want to stand in the way of both of us surrendering our hearts to God? Definitely not. I think this is a case where God used a bad situation to bring about His glory and I wouldn't want to wish that undone," he said. "At this point, our energy is better spent focusing on what we have here, today, and on what tomorrow could be."

As much as she would have loved to have had him around the last five years, she knew he was right and she told him so.

Cassidy tried putting weight on her leg and found it didn't hurt too badly. Besides, nothing was going to keep her from making it to the top. She had her parental pride to maintain. If she chickened out, Piper would never let her hear the end of it.

They didn't talk much as they entered the steeper part of the journey, but Wade stayed close by. Cassidy found herself praying for the first time in over a week. She asked God to forgive her for doubting Him and also prayed about the future, asking Him to guide her steps.

And her heart.

With Cassidy's fall, it had taken longer to reach the top than normal. Not that Wade had minded. More time alone with Cassidy was not a problem where he was concerned. When they reached the top, Piper spotted them first and jogged over to hug both of them.

"We beat you guys by a hundred years." She pulled

away. "Do you have snacks? Because I could use a snack."

Cassidy and Wade both laughed. Wade turned his back toward Cassidy, so she could unzip the pack and find something for Piper to eat. The simple action filled Wade with longing for this to be his everyday life. He wanted his family. Not just for little planned adventures or seeing each other at the ranch—he wanted to live together. Do life together. Live as a family.

He wanted them. Like this. Forever.

Was he foolish to pray that was possible?

Shannon waved them over to a prime spot on the western side of the rock. "Seven minutes until sunset by my calculations. And by that I mean I looked up today's sunset time online earlier." She stretched out her legs as they took seats beside her. "Anyone else's calves on fire?"

"Fire?" Cassidy snorted. "Pure lava."

Shannon thrust her wrist in Wade's face. "My Fitbit says I climbed sixty flights of stairs. Sixty. That's how steep this rock is. Who knew?"

"I did." Wade raised his hand. "Park ranger, remember?"

Piper unceremoniously plopped herself into Wade's lap. "Did you know my birthday is coming up? I'm turning five. That's a whole hand and I already know how to spell it too." She demonstrated her skill for him. "I'm going to have a cowgirl birthday party with a bounce house and everything."

"That sounds amazing." Wade handed Piper a water bottle and urged her to drink more.

She took a long sip, then dragged the back of her arm across her lips. "You'll come to my party, won't you?"

"Of course, I'll be there." Wade tucked his arm around her and pointed to steer her attention toward the horizon. The sky was a brilliant deep purple-pink laced with wisps of white clouds. Stunning Texas Hill Country land spanned out in greens and blues and yellows as far as the eye could see. The world seemed to go on forever from where they were and it made Wade feel very small.

Before he had been diagnosed with cancer, he could have appreciated a scene like this one. Even called it pretty. He had witnessed a lifetime's worth of spectacular sunsets from boats in the Caribbean. But this one surpassed anything he had ever seen. Surrounded by people he loved while the truth of how quickly life could change, how quickly his own health could be stolen away rested heavily on him; he had to fight back a well of emotion. The God who had taken the time to craft such amazing beauty had also created him and had given Wade a second chance. If the surgery went well, he could even call it a third chance.

And he refused to squander it.

Wade turned his attention to Cassidy. Her face was a mask of intensity as she watched the sunset. Wade's mouth went dry. Sweat- and dirt-streaked, with hairs falling loose from her ponytail, she was honestly the most beautiful person he had ever seen.

Back on the trail after doctoring her, if he had leaned in after she had brushed the hair off his forehead, he could have kissed her. Probably should have. If he had, would things have changed between them?

As much as he wanted that, he told himself he was glad nothing had happened. He needed to wait until after his surgery. After he had received a clean bill of health. After he was at a point where being in her life wouldn't equate to being a complete burden.

But as his gaze tripped over Cassidy's petite features, he prayed that they could reconcile completely. He prayed that the day to kiss her would come sooner rather than later.

A gasp whooshed out of Piper as she nestled against him. "This is so pretty."

"It is, Piper," Wade said. "It really is."

Soon after the sun dipped below the horizon, Piper dozed off. Shannon filled Cassidy and Wade in on the caves they had explored while they were waiting for them to reach the top. Then she shifted to telling Cassidy about Cord.

"I broke things off," Shannon said.

"For good?" Cassidy reached out and took Shannon's hand.

Shannon nodded. "It was a long time coming."

"I'm so happy for you and I'm so proud of you. There's someone out there who will treat you better," Cassidy said.

Shannon gave a sad smile. "Who knows? But for now, *I* have to treat me better. And not being with him is a piece of that."

Wade was glad Shannon was trusting someone besides him. Rhett would need to be told soon too since the ranch was listed in the protection order.

When it was time to head back down, Cassidy pressed her fingertips to Piper's face. "It's a shame to wake her," she whispered. "I'm sure she's tuckered out. She's never up this late."

Wade shook his head. "I'll carry her." Despite the sun setting, the lights from the parking lot and along the trail were enough to see by.

Cassidy stopped him on his way to pick Piper up. "It's too steep for that. What if you fall?"

"He's always been as sure-footed as a goat." Shannon flapped her hand. "He'll be fine. And we can stick close in case he needs help."

"Fine. But only because she would probably fall on her own, as tired as she is." Cassidy held out her hand. "But I'm taking the backpack."

Wade relented. Cassidy dug a flashlight from the backpack and clicked it on before slinging the bag onto her shoulders. In the wash of her flashlight, they started back down the rock face.

Back toward home.

Chapter Nine

After their trip to Enchanted Rock, the next week flew by. The first wave of campers descended upon the Jarretts' property and Wade was reminded of how much he cared about the mission of Red Dog Ranch. His father had been dedicated to meeting the needs of foster children and foster families, and Wade was relieved to see that his brother had continued the tradition.

Wade yanked off his work glove, flexed his fingers, then dragged his hand down his face. Sweat clung to every part of his body and he was positive Piper would declare that he stunk if she bumped into him anytime soon.

He couldn't help but smile when his daughter crossed his mind. She was a little firecracker who constantly kept him on his toes, and he thanked God for her every heartbeat he could. Since their trip to Enchanted Rock, Cassidy had been inviting Wade into their family more and more. Most nights, he was there to help tuck Piper into bed. He would stop by for popcorn and movies with them and they both teased him relentlessly for falling asleep on the couch five or six minutes into the show each time. Piper sought him out each day to play a board game and so far she had won most of them and she wasn't about to let him forget that fact.

He wouldn't have wanted it any other way.

He had also been stopping his work outside earlier in order to shower, then head to the dining hall to help Cassidy with dinner cleanup. Now that there were campers, she had more responsibilities and he wanted to lessen her load any way he could. Even with the help of her two teenage kitchen helpers, it could take hours.

He rose from the crouched position he had been working in for far too long, his legs wobbling with the effort. He took a deep breath. If he didn't start sleeping better, he wouldn't be able to keep up these hours.

In an effort to forget his upcoming surgery, Wade had thrown himself into rebuilding another one of the cabins. There were only three left and he was determined to complete them even if he had to do it alone.

It hadn't made him forget he had cancer, but he still found it valuable to fill all his waking hours, zapping his energy so he couldn't worry as much.

Rhett, Macy and Shannon had become scarce around the Jarrett home, as they were fully involved with running the camp session. They were often on the go, planning and running all activities for the campers from six in the morning until nine at night. Since the cabins weren't all completed yet, Rhett had been forced to limit the number of campers they could take and wait-list some of the kids. Wade knew it bothered Rhett to have to do it; it bothered Wade too.

Wade made a point to check in on his mom whenever

he took a break. His siblings were busy and he enjoyed spending time with her. He had to admit though, in the last week her bad days had outweighed her good ones. The new night nurse had started two evenings ago and so far that seemed to be helping. But he wished there was more they could do for their mom.

"You look worn down," Rhett's voice boomed from behind Wade.

Wade grabbed hold of one of the boards he had just installed to frame out the doorway. He leaned on it as he faced his brother. Kodiak, his brother's ever-present shadow, sat a foot from Rhett, her adoring eyes trained on her master.

Wade pushed his free hand into the small of his back and gave an exaggerated groan. "Guess I'm not as young as I used to be."

Rhett's lips ticked up a fraction. "Careful, I've got more than five years on you so if you're old, I'm ancient. Not exactly what a man wants to hear this close to his wedding."

When Wade first learned Rhett and Macy had planned their wedding to happen in the middle of their summer programs, he had questioned their sanity. Why would they willingly enter into such a big, new part of their journey together when their lives were at the busiest? Fall was only months away and surely they could hold off until then. They had so much going on they wouldn't be able to take a honeymoon until the end of the season. His brother had usually been so rational and the wedding date seemed to be the least rational choice ever.

But now with Cassidy—Wade understood completely. If he were in a better place, if he had more of his ducks in a row, if Cassidy could ever love him again...well, he would rush a wedding too.

Wade hooked a hand over his shoulder and squeezed at the knots there. "Good thing Macy keeps you young and on your toes."

His brother laughed. "That she does. But I didn't come here to talk about me."

Of course he hadn't. Always the most introverted of the Jarrett siblings, Rhett wasn't one to seek out chit-chat. Rhett was the brother who fully embodied the cowboy way—quiet, strong, always in a hat and boots. His button-down forever neatly tucked in with his belt buckle glinting in the sunlight. He had turned out to be a carbon copy of their father.

Rhett hooked his thumbs in his pockets and studied the fence line. The muscles in his jaw popped and Kodiak gave a little whine. Wade waited for his brother to speak.

Rhett's Adam's apple bobbed. "I haven't been very welcoming to you and I'm sorry about that. You're family. You belong here. And you're welcome here."

Wade lowered his shaking legs to sit on the floor with his feet dangling off the elevated porch. He knew how hard that had been for Rhett to say.

"Thank you for that."

Rhett's long stride ate up the space between them until he was standing a few feet in front of Wade. "That's not all I have to say." Rhett looked away again. "You saved Shannon from that monster when I couldn't." He scrubbed a hand over his forehead, setting his hat askew. "And even if I had, I wouldn't have handled it as well as you did. I would have wanted to hunt Cord down and deal with him myself."

"Oh, I wanted to do that too," Wade said. "But I figured getting him a record was a better long-term solution that could hopefully help more women than just Shannon."

Rhett ran his fingers across his jaw. "Before you returned, I tried to save her and I went about it all wrong, and she suffered for longer than she ever should have because I couldn't reach her."

Wade sighed. "That's not true, Rhett. She probably wasn't ready when you tried. With these things, it has to be the person's decision or they'll go back. Shannon was finally ready when I talked to her. She hadn't been before. Neither of us saved or rescued her. She did that really well herself once she had the tools and momentum."

"I don't know." Rhett crossed his arm. "You two have always had this connection the rest of us couldn't tap into."

Kodiak must have realized this talk was going longer than Rhett's normal interactions because she flopped onto the ground with a loud huff.

"We're twins." Wade shrugged. "I don't know what to say."

"It's more than that," Rhett said. "I— There's more I have to tell you."

"This is the day for confessions, huh?"

"You know me." A small grin lit his brother's usually serious features. "I better get them all out while I feel like it or who knows how long it would take me to come clean with you."

"Come clean?" That sounded ominous.

"After the tornado hit, there was damage in the office. It opened up this secret compartment in the wall."

"Consider me intrigued."

Rhett brushed his hand over a smirk. It vanished just as quickly when he let out a shaky breath. "The compartment held a family secret. Namely that I was adopted."

Adopted? Wade had to have heard wrong. Hadn't he just been thinking about how Rhett was a carbon copy of their father?

"Are you sure?"

"Positive." Rhett fidgeted with his hat. "I have all the proof if you want to see it."

"It's just..." Wade used his hand to encompass all of Rhett. "You're the most Jarrett out of all of us."

"I can show you the paperwork."

"I believe you." Wade held his hands up in surrender. "I just think it's amazing that God placed you into our family. You're this perfect fit and from what I hear, you've held us together when the rest of us would have failed."

Never comfortable with flattery, Rhett cast his gaze to the Texas dirt. "Anyway, I told you that because I wanted you to know I forgive you for everything. For letting us think you were dead. Shannon told me why you did it and I'm sorry if anything I did or said ever made you feel unwanted or like you were a disappointment—you never were, Wade." His gaze cut to Wade's—intense and earnest. "We just wanted to save you the same way we have all wanted to step in and help Shannon. Because we loved you and wanted the best for your life. And, well,

I wanted you to know about the adoption because I've been keeping that from you since you got back and it was wrong of me to be upset with you for keeping something from us when I was keeping something from you."

Now was the time when he should tell Rhett why he needed the day off on Friday and why he may need most of next week off too. *Oh, Rhett, by the way, I have surgery on Friday. It's for cancer. Yeah, I've known for some time but I didn't tell you.*

Wade braced himself. He opened his mouth—

Rhett's phone blared out a Clint Oakfield song and he answered it. "Hey, beautiful. Yeah, I can be there in two. Love you. Yup, on my way."

A few minutes later, as Wade hobbled toward the Jarrett house, Shannon intercepted him. She hooked her arm through his and dragged him toward the barn.

"Watch the bicep." He shrugged away from her. "I'm sore."

Shannon rolled her eyes. "I've been trying to catch you when we both had a second alone all week. We need to talk."

He rubbed his arm. His muscles burned from overuse. "You and Rhett and everyone else."

"I keep hearing Piper say you're going to be at her birthday party."

"Because I am."

"It's four days after your surgery, Wade." She jammed a finger into his ribs. "Do you honestly think that's a good idea?" She poked his chest as she delivered each word.

He lightly batted her hand away. "The doctor said I should be up and around within two or three days. You were there when he said it. Piper's birthday is four days after my surgery, so I should be fine." He would have a scar and possibly still have a bandage on his neck, but those were things that could be covered up with some creativity.

Shannon put her hands up, fingers curled as if she would like to give him a good shake. "He said you *could* be up in two to three days if you end up having a best-case-scenario situation."

"Which is what I'm praying for."

"Me too. But, Wade, what if that doesn't happen?" She crossed her arms and glared at him. "You have to tell them what's going on."

"I am not dropping the *C* word on people eight days before Piper's birthday," he said. "Do you know how much of a damper that would be? Cassidy and Piper are both so excited. I won't take that from them."

He wouldn't worry them. Wouldn't do anything to lessen their excitement. It would be selfish to take the attention off Piper and off the camp sessions. He could handle this with God like he had planned. Wasn't that how a believer showed faith?

Shannon's voice was a low rumble. "If you love them as much as you act like you do, you would trust them with this part of you."

"It has nothing to do with trust."

"Keep telling yourself that. I'm sure it helps." She pursed her lips as if she wanted to keep drilling into him but instead she asked, "What are you doing with your Thursday?"

The ranch was currently hosting some of their youngest campers so instead of the normal four- or five-day camp session, this one was only three. After they left on Wednesday night, Rhett had declared Thursday would be a paid day off for everyone at the ranch—a thank-you for all the hard work and long hours they had poured into the ranch in order to get it ready for summer. The staff would reconvene on Friday to clean up and get the ranch ready for next week's campers.

"I'm taking Cassidy and Piper to Gorman Falls."

"Perfect. So you can tell them then." So they were back to this. That hadn't taken long.

The day before the surgery. "It's a little late at that point."

"Just promise me you'll consider telling them. They deserve to know."

He blew out a long breath. "I'll consider it."

For Shannon's sake, he would give it a little more thought.

Chapter Ten

Cassidy wasn't ready on Thursday when Wade knocked on her front door. To be fair, she didn't think it was possible that she would ever get over the thrill that ran through her when she knew Wade was on the other side of the door.

The love she had thought she had lost.

The love she was finding again.

She wouldn't deny it any longer. Cassidy was falling for this new version of Wade harder than she had ever fallen for the old one—and that was saying a lot. But this Wade was driven in a way he had never been as a teenager and he was dedicated, thoughtful and always willing to help. He was a great dad. He had been nothing but open and honest with her and Piper. They could be a family again if Cassidy was willing to put her heart out there.

Was she?

Cassidy opened the front door to find Wade standing there, smiling at her with a bunch of black-eyed Susans in his hands. He stepped inside and she took the flowers from him. They had always been her favorites, which was why she had planted some at his gravesite a few years ago. Had he visited the cemetery and seen them there?

She arranged them in a vase on her counter. "I have some bad news for you."

Wade cocked his head. "Don't tell me you guys are standing me up."

"You're half right. Macy called in to a radio station last night and won tickets to Dinosaur Expedition. It's this traveling show with life-size moving dinosaurs. It's actually supposed to be pretty fun. She took Piper with her this morning. I'm sorry."

"If I'm going to be ditched, at least it was for something as cool as dinosaurs." Wade's laugh was rich and warm, like honey in hot tea. "But you're coming, right?"

"You still want to go?" Cassidy held her breath after she asked the question. She had worried that he wouldn't be interested if Piper wasn't there. He might have only been spending time with Cassidy because he wanted a relationship with his daughter.

It wasn't one of his almost-smiles that graced his features; it was a full-blown lightens-every-plane-and-angle sort of smile. "Of course."

They were on the road within minutes. Cassidy relaxed into the seat, happy to trust Wade to drive them wherever.

Wade adjusted the air-conditioning. "I've noticed you don't have any pictures of your parents at your place."

Cassidy stiffened. She was fine with Wade asking about her folks, but she always braced a little when she had to talk about them. "That's because they kicked me out of the house and told me not to come back."

"Piper?" Wade breathed.

"You know how they were." Cassidy had grown up as the only child in an upper middle-class home. The Danverses had been suburbanites in a school district of mostly farmers. Her parents were suite holders at McLane Stadium even though they rarely made the trek to attend a Baylor game. They were members at the golf club and her mother regularly hosted teas for the local chapter of the Daughters of the Republic of Texas. They'd had high hopes that Cassidy would grow up to be someone worthy of fawning over. They had spent Cassidy's entire life pressuring her and telling her what she was and wasn't allowed to do and who she was and wasn't allowed to talk to. Their strictness had driven her toward Wade.

She hugged her stomach. "When they found out I was pregnant, they wanted me to terminate the pregnancy." Thankfully she had turned eighteen the month before, so they couldn't force her to obey their wishes as much as they could have if she had still been a juvenile. "They said Piper was a mistake that would ruin my life." A derisive laugh ripped from Cassidy. "Joke's on them. Piper's the best thing that ever happened to me."

Wade quickly glanced her way, probably assessing how she was doing with their talk. "They kicked you out?"

"They disowned me. That was my mother's choice word the last time we talked. *If you don't do this we are officially disowning you,*" she mimicked her mother's stern voice.

"Is there an unofficial way to disown someone?"

"I think that's called ghosting." Which looked like what Wade had done to them, but she decided she wouldn't point that out. They were moving on. She understood his reasons and forgave him.

"They tried to bribe me, Wade." That might have been the part that still bothered her the most. As if she had been a child clinging to a lollipop that they didn't want her to have instead of a child. They tried to make a trade. The thought made her stomach roll. "They told me if I had an abortion, they would pay for college and I could study anything, anywhere I wanted." They presented it to her as if they were making some huge gracious concession because before they had dictated two or three degrees she had to choose between.

Cassidy hugged her stomach tighter. "They said they wouldn't tell anyone what I had done, so I could still have the *hope for a good future*. But if I kept the child, if I went through *with this*—their words—they said they wouldn't support me and didn't want to know the child. So I left. I haven't talked to them since."

Wade's hand touched her arm, his fingers slipped down until he was able to take hold of her fingers. She relaxed her shoulders and uncrossed her arms, so she could wrap his hand inside both of hers and hold it in her lap.

Cassidy pressed on. "Rhett stopped by my parents' house to check on me and I told him what was going on. He helped me pack my stuff and moved me to the ranch that day."

"I owe Rhett so much," Wade said. "Shannon had hinted to me that you were estranged from your parents, but I had no idea. I'm so sorry you had to go through that."

She ran her fingers over his knuckles. Traced a scar on the back of his hand and wondered where it had come from. "It still hurts, you know? To know my own parents didn't want me—didn't want our beautiful child. All because their status was more important to them. I tell myself I'm better off without them, but the rejection still cuts when I think about it. Like was a teen pregnancy really the worst thing that could have happened to me?"

"I can't imagine what that must be like." Wade's voice was quiet. "My family. They're so different."

"They're perfect," Cassidy said. "Your family is perfect."

"You realize that includes you too. You're family, Cass." His fingers tightened on hers. "You're my family."

Cassidy swallowed hard as she looked out the window. The browns, yellows and greens of Texas Hill Country flashed by her as they rolled on. Wade was right. They were a family.

And maybe one day, the three of them would be able to make that official.

Wade adjusted the pack he wore and then took Cassidy's hand again. They continued down the path. He had forgotten how challenging the hike to Gorman Falls could be. It was a mile and a half over rugged terrain. Not that Cassidy seemed to mind. Despite their conversation about hard things in the car, she had been smiling the whole hike.

She released his hand and got close to the bank of the river. A couple of frogs protested her presence and splashed into the water. Wade stayed back and watched as she flipped over rocks and shoved aside sticks with her shoes.

"Lose something?"

She kept her focus on the river. "Remember when we used to find topaz in the riverbeds?" Cassidy squatted down and flipped another rock. She pulled a face and wiped her fingers on her jeans.

Wade nodded. "But if you find it here, you're not allowed to bring it home. State park rules."

"Of course, Ranger." She saluted him the same way Shannon had at Enchanted Rock.

"Watch out," he called as her hand hovered close to the water's surface. "You don't want an alligator gar to think your hand is food."

"Oh, come on." She splashed water in his direction. "You've been feeding me a line about that fish since I was twelve and I've never seen one in this river." She rose and popped her hands to her hips. "Actually, I've never seen one at all. Besides, I'm pretty sure they feed at night, Wade."

He shook his finger at her, enjoying the tease in her voice. "Just because you haven't seen one, doesn't mean it's not there."

She marched toward him, her eyes narrowed. "You're just trying to scare me." She put her hands on his chest and gave a playful push. "Aren't you?"

"Is it working?" He grinned down at her. "Because if you're afraid, I'm completely fine with you clinging to me. You know, for protection."

Cassidy bit her lip as she walked her fingers up his chest. "Only for protection, huh? You don't want me clinging to you for any other reason?"

"Cass." Her name was a whispered warning, letting her know he wouldn't be able to hold back if she kept this up.

Cassidy inched closer, sliding her arms around his waist. Her hands found a resting spot at the small of his back under the backpack he wore. "So you're willing to protect me from alligator gar." She tipped her head up and looked at him. Even batted her eyelashes. "Anything else?"

When they had dated, Cassidy had loved to flirt with him and he had loved how confident she was when she teased him. But she was walking a dangerous line. They couldn't flirt like this and then act like it hadn't happened.

Wade set his hands on her shoulders. He licked his lips. "I'll protect you from anything, Cass. From everything."

"What about from you?" she whispered.

He opened his mouth, not sure how to answer. Not sure what she meant.

"Promise you won't ever leave again." She slipped a hand between them to press a finger to his lips. "But if you promise me that, you better be ready to kiss me."

Wade couldn't take it any longer. He tugged her hand away from his face so there would be nothing between them. Then he claimed her lips. He had meant for it to be a slow kiss, but Cassidy's hand was instantly in his hair and her nails dragged against his scalp and he couldn't help but deepen the kiss. It was as if they were each other's oxygen and they'd been dying to take a full breath for years.

Cassidy was in his arms again and it felt right. He didn't want to let go.

Promise you won't ever leave again.

Never. He would never leave this woman for as long

as he lived. He would dedicate the rest of his life to making her happy and meeting her needs.

When they finally parted, they leaned against each other, almost as if they would fall down without support. Wade's legs trembled and his pulse crashed through him as if he had run a marathon. Cassidy hugged his middle again and pressed her head against his chest, her shoulders rising with ragged breaths. Wade wrapped his arms around her and rested the side of his head against the top of hers.

Wade had promised Shannon he would consider telling Cassidy about the surgery tomorrow. His sister had urged him again yesterday when she had helped him move some of his belongings into an empty staff house at the ranch, so he could stay there until he was healed enough to be in public. Coming back to the Jarrett house wasn't an option. If his mom or Rhett spotted him, they would be worried, which was why he had already told them he would be away for the weekend to take care of some things.

Tonight after he dropped Cassidy off, he would have to turn around and drive to Houston and check into a hotel room so he could be at the hospital bright and early in the morning. After what he and Cassidy had just shared, he was beginning to think Shannon might have a point. When they got to the falls, he would tell her.

After a few minutes, they reluctantly untwined from their hug.

Wade offered his hand. "We did come to see the main attraction, right?"

Cassidy laughed softly. "I don't know. I kind of thought we just had the main attraction for the day."

They continued down the path, walking a little closer than necessary. They stole a few more quick kisses as they walked. Wade's mind buzzed with questions. Did this mean they were dating again? He wanted to discuss it but wanted to wait until after she knew about his thyroid cancer. It was only fair.

Cassidy brushed past so she was ahead of him on a narrow part of the path, towing him by the hand in her wake. "You haven't said much about what you were up to before you came back. On the way to Enchanted Rock, Piper asked where you had been and I noticed you didn't answer that part."

Wade heaved a breath. "I didn't want to explain to Piper what a party boat was or what happened on one."

"Will you explain to me?"

Wade passed Cassidy in order to hold some branches out of their way. She ducked under them and he followed.

"They're these luxury yachts that the wealthy rent out," he said. "Depending on the boat, they pay anywhere from 40K to 100K a week to stay on these things. And with that type of money comes this expectation that their every whim will be catered to. If they want wine flown in from Italy brought to them in bed at two in the morning, you do it. When we had guests, you're basically on duty twenty-four hours a day."

And sometimes the female guests tried to throw themselves at the deckhands. Wade wouldn't mention that part. He had never had an interest in any of them and thankfully the main boat he had worked on had a no-fraternizing-with-the-guests policy that saved them from most advances. Sticking with Preach, who was an expert at diverting their attention elsewhere, had also saved Wade from his share of awkward advances through the years.

Cassidy pursed her lips. "That doesn't sound like the best situation for someone to be in if they're trying to overcome an addiction."

It had pretty much been the worst place he could have been. Though in the end, Wade believed God's hand was in where he ended up because facing down the hard temptations had made him stronger.

"It wasn't. Those people drank from sunup to sundown. Massive quantities. My saving grace was I was pretty depressed from being away from you, and my bunkmate on my first trip was Preach." And thankfully whenever it had been time to find a new boat to work on, Preach had come along with him.

"That's his name?"

"No, his real name is Elochukwu. He's Nigerian. But he told us to call him Preach. That man loved God and he wasn't afraid to talk to the staff about it. At first, I was so angry with him." Wade had even begged the captain to move him to another room. "He would quote Bible verses at me while we were on our hands and knees scrubbing the decks. He would sing hymns in our bunk at night. He slowly wore me down though and became a good friend. Preach led me to the Lord after eight months of working on me."

"It sounds like a weird job for him to have too."

"Preach had a family back in Nigeria. A wife and three kids," Wade said. "He was there because we were paid really well and at the end of the week, the renter usually tipped the staff in cash. Depending on who it was, it could be a ten-thousand-dollar tip left to split between us." Without many expenses, Wade had squirreled most of the money away over the years, which was the only reason he had been able to pay the medical bills so far. If Wade hadn't stockpiled his tips, he would have been forced to confide in Rhett by now for help.

"Preach sent most of it home. He's trying to build a church in his community and he didn't want help from an outside organization to do it. He said God called him to take care of his village." Wade shrugged. "I thought it was really cool. He reminded me a lot of Boone."

"Ironic because you and Boone were never too close."

Cassidy was right about that. Boone had been so book smart and straight edge, they just hadn't had much in common when they were younger. When Wade had begged Boone to help him learn to be a bull rider, Boone had shoved him off to go to the library to study. When Wade wanted a sibling to go exploring with him, Boone rolled his eyes and told him to go find Shannon.

"True. But I have a feeling we could be friends now if we were given the chance."

Wade sent up a prayer that he and Boone could patch up their relationship. *Please let my calls go through next time.*

They reached the last one hundred yards of the hike, which consisted of a rocky slope down a steep path into clouds of mist gathering from half a dozen cascades spilling off the sixty-foot limestone cliff. The chilled air that clung to them as they descended the path was refreshing after their brisk hike. At the bottom, they were greeted by a moss-and-fern-swathed grotto. Every rock in sight had patches of green. For the moment, they were alone at the falls. They found a large rock near the bottom and huddled together there. Cassidy pulled her knees up to her chest and laid her head on them. They sat like that in silence for a little while. Content to just be together.

Tell her now. Before you lose your nerve. Now.

"Cassidy—"

"If we're going to do this, I think I need to wrap you in bubble wrap or something," she blurted out. "That's the only way this is going to work."

"Wait." Wade crinkled his brow. "Bubble wrap? What are you talking about?"

She twisted toward him and latched onto his wrist with a fierceness that made him wonder if she thought he might disappear right here.

"I don't think my heart could take it if something happened to you again. Don't you understand?" Her eyes searched his face. "I lost you once." Only a whisper but it completely gutted him.

"I'm right here." He cupped her face.

She leaned into his hand. "I know what it feels like to lose you. I'd be lying if I said I'm not terrified right now." She sat up, letting his hand fall away. "What if I let myself care about you in that way and you get hit by a car like your dad was? What if something happens to you, Wade?" Her eyes went wide. She sucked in a deep breath. Closed her eyes. "You're going to have to be patient with me. I'm afraid I might worry or freak out for a while whenever you're late to something or if there is a chance of you getting hurt. It's something I'm going to have to work on but I think it may take a long time."

Her words were a band around his chest, around his lungs, that pulled tighter and tighter until Wade was afraid he would have to gasp for air. Thickness gathered at the back of his throat.

He couldn't tell her about his surgery.

Given what she had just admitted, revealing he had cancer would scare her. He would have to follow his original plan. Just have the surgery done and she would never have to know, never have to deal with yet another thing that could cause her anguish. The doctor had explained to Wade that the type of cancer he had been diagnosed with had the highest survival rate out of any cancer. Wade would face down the monster tomorrow, overcome it, then pursue Cassidy without anything holding him back.

One last hurdle. He could do this.

But first, he needed to reassure Cassidy before he was away from her for three days. She knew he had to go to Houston but he had given vague reasons. Just that he had some unfinished business to take care of. When she had pressed and asked what sort of business, he had told her it wasn't a big deal. Now that she had spelled out her fears, he didn't want her doubting anything.

Wade wrapped his arms around Cassidy, dragging her to him. "I love you." His voice cracked. "I never stopped."

She nuzzled against his neck and pressed a kiss to his skin there. "I love you too, Wade. I always have. I always will."

Chapter Eleven

Wade tried to get up from his chair but a sharp slash of fire raced through his neck and back, traveling up into his head. He gasped. Musty air from the usually unoccupied staff house filled his lungs. He suffered through a few coughs that sent blades of pain through his body.

He tried to lift his arm to see his watch but couldn't. The doctor had warned him that they had cut deeper into his side to remove more lymph nodes than they had initially planned. He would be sore and it would possibly be a while until he could lift his arms higher than mid-torso.

Wade closed his eyes against a wince. He didn't need the clock to confirm what day it was. He had spent Friday and Saturday in the hospital. When they released him on Saturday evening, Shannon had stayed with him at a hotel in Houston to give him another day to heal before the long car trip home. She had driven him back to the ranch late on Sunday night, helping him into the staff house when they were sure no one would see them. He had spent Monday alone in the house, sucking on ice shards while he waited to feel better.

The feeling better part? It had never happened.

Now it was Tuesday.

Day four. Piper's birthday.

He *had* to get up.

"God, please." His voice was hoarse from disuse. "Please give me the strength to get up."

It wasn't supposed to be like this. He was supposed to be up and around by now. He was supposed to feel fine. His team of doctors had shared stories with him about patients who went to the movies on day three or four. Or had coffee with friends by now. Out. Among the world. But Wade couldn't get up from a chair without what felt like a herculean amount of effort.

A tremor went through his body. Had Shannon cranked his air-conditioning when she checked on him this morning? He was freezing.

The front door clicked open and he lifted his lids to see Shannon. She strode closer and frowned. "You still look horrible."

"Thanks, sis." He coughed and it hurt. Man, it hurt. So much.

She bent near and pressed her hand to his forehead. "No fever. So probably no infection. At least you have that working for you."

Wade sucked in a quick tight breath. "I need you to help me get up and get ready for Piper's party."

She set a hand on his shoulder and applied pressure. "You're not going anywhere."

"I have to, Shannon. If I'm not there— I promised Piper. I told Cassidy I wouldn't let either of them down." But here he was letting them down, being the disappointment he had always been. Everyone would be left to mutter "older Wade, same shenanigans."

Why hadn't he insisted on putting off the surgery until after Piper's party? His doctor had presented a great argument for the quick surgery, but it had been Wade's health at stake. He could have put it off.

He *should* have put it off.

Wade imagined waiting and learning that cancer cells had infected more lymph nodes or moved elsewhere. Taken over the other side of his thyroid. No, he couldn't regret getting it out as rapidly as he had but the timing was horrible to say the least.

But they told him he would be fine by day four. He had counted on it.

"Maybe you should have told her what you were going through, then there wouldn't be a big fallout over you not showing up." She yanked a phone from her back pocket. "You could just give her a call." She jiggled the phone near his face. "But if you do, she is going to want an explanation." She tucked her phone back away. "And what would you tell her, Wade? What would you say?"

"It wasn't supposed to be like this. They had said I'd be fine in two or three days."

"Yeah, well, I called and talked to them and they said you could be healing slower if you were run-down before the surgery. Which, let's be honest, you were."

"I hadn't slept a full night in a month."

"On top of that, you were working yourself to the bone."

"There were things to do." He hadn't been able to finish the cabins in time. He hoped Rhett could find someone else to finish them before they were needed later in the summer for campers.

"Well, I know for sure you've slept through the night for at least the last two or three nights. Keep it up and you'll be able to be up and around soon. If not, we'll ask at your appointment on Friday."

"I'm going to sit up. It hurts, but I can do it." He braced his arms on the armrests. He had been getting up on his own to grab snacks and things like that when Shannon wasn't around. It was just he preferred to save it for when movement was absolutely necessary. With a grunt and a jerky movement that did nothing to ebb his pain, Wade shoved to his feet. The muscles running along his neck and shoulders screamed in protest. He grabbed onto a nearby table to steady himself as he wheezed out a breath.

He wasn't used to being weak. No control over what he could and couldn't do.

Shannon shook her head. "I really think you should just sit back down and take it easy." Belying her words, Shannon came to his side and wrapped an arm around his waist for support. They walked around the room twice and then she helped him sit at the overhang of the kitchen counter while she fished things out of the fridge to make a sandwich.

Wade traced a swirl in the countertop. "Maybe I could make a quick appearance?"

"Please, Wade, be serious." She pointed a butter knife at him. A glob of mayonnaise slid off and plopped onto the counter a foot away. "Even if you hobbled over to the party, people are going to take one look at you and know you're not okay and there will be questions. Your bandage is bigger than I thought it would be." She gestured at his neck. "You would have to rock a winter scarf to hide it. Do you even own a winter scarf?" She held up a hand. "Don't even answer that. Let's pretend

you were able to disguise all of that." She made a circle
motion at her neck. "What are you going to do when
Piper throws herself at you? You do understand that
would be unavoidable, right? It's her *birthday*, Wade.
You're her dad and she hasn't seen you since last week.
She's going to fling herself at you."

"You're right," Wade said. He wanted to drop his
head into his hands, but the movement would have hurt
too much. "I don't like it, but you're right."

Piper would want him to hug her and pick her up and
he was in no condition to do so. It would hurt his daughter's feelings if he brushed her off when she jumped at
him. And Cassidy would notice something was wrong
with him the second she caught sight of him.

His phone pinged with an incoming message.

Shannon twisted to stare at where his phone rested
on the little table near the reclining chair he had been
sleeping in. "Want me to go get it for you?"

"Thank you."

Shannon slid a sandwich in front of him and then
went and got his phone. She set it next to the plate. "You
know this is going to be Cassidy. The party starts in
minutes and she's going to be asking where you are."

Wade punched in his password and sure enough,
there was a text from Cassidy.

You should have been here an hour ago. Where are
you?

Wade stared at the screen for a second. He could
tell her the truth now, but that would ruin Piper's day.
And to what end? If the doctors proclaimed him to be

cancer free on Friday, then he would have worried her for nothing.

He typed back.

I won't make it. I'm so so so so so so so so sorry.

He shot off a second text right after that one.

I'll make this up to her. We can go away to a waterpark. A whole weekend of celebrating.

Cassidy was quick to shoot back, This is unacceptable. Get here. Now.

Wade sighed.

I'm sick today.

His phone rattled.

Are you contagious?

Wade closed his eyes for a heartbeat. He wouldn't lie to her.

Not contagious. Just feel awful. You know I'd be there if I could. Tell Piper I love her.

Cassidy's response took longer this time, but then a bunch came through in quick secession.

She needs you!
You can stop by, even if you're sick.

Do you know how often I've had to do things when I was sick? It's called being a parent!
You PROMISED you would come.
This is NOT ok.

Wade silenced his phone and set it on the cushion of the chair next to where he was sitting. Text messages could be misunderstood and often made things worse. He would have to wait this situation out until the weekend, after he had been to see his doctors and had answers. At that point his bandage should be removed, and he had looked up pictures online—the scar wouldn't look too bad. It shouldn't frighten Piper by then.

Shannon still stood on the other side of the island, eyebrows raised. "You gonna enlighten me?"

"Please tell Cassidy that I have a really good, completely legitimate reason for not being there. Please, Shannon. I'm begging you to help me. She had only just warmed up to us being together again and I don't want to ruin anything."

"Well, you know what I would say to that."

"I already ruined it by not telling her."

"Look at you. Quick learner." She came over and wrapped him in a gentle hug. "I'll check on you later and I'll make excuses as good as I can."

After she left, Wade made his way back to the recliner. He glanced at his phone again and debated calling Cassidy and setting things right, but he decided against it. The truth would take attention away from Piper on her special day and he wasn't about to lie, so that left him with nothing to say. For now. Still, he stared at the screen until his eyes went heavy. His medication must have been kicking in.

It wasn't supposed to happen like this. He was supposed to feel fine today.

The phone slipped from his hand as he fell asleep.

Cassidy prowled through the yard, surveying Piper's birthday party in full swing.

Purple balloons bobbed along the fence nearest the Jarrett house. Sheep, Piper's pony, watched them suspiciously while Romeo, the miniature donkey who shared Sheep's enclosure, seemed as if he couldn't have cared less. The giant bounce house and inflatable obstacle courses were packed with kids from her preschool, as well as kids from the foster program who Piper had befriended. Cloudstorm stalked near the row of tables where food was piled.

By all accounts, the party was going well.

Except the birthday girl had teared up twice already, looking for her dad.

"Is he here yet?" she asked the second she spotted Cassidy again. "When will he be here?"

Cassidy crouched in front of her. "Your dad isn't able to make it, sweetheart."

Piper's lip quivered. "But he said he would. He told me he would." A fat tear skated down her cheek.

Cassidy framed her daughter's face so she could wipe away the tears. "I know he did. Sometimes things come up."

"He said nothing would keep him away."

Cassidy pulled Piper into a hug and held her like that for a few minutes. She kissed the top of her head.

"Look at all these people who are here to celebrate your special day." She fanned her hand to indicate the party. "They all love you and want to spend time with you."

Piper kicked at the ground. "I wanted to celebrate as a family."

Cassidy pointed out Rhett in the crowd. "Your uncle is looking for you. Go say hi to him for me, will you? Hang out with him until I come get you."

Piper's bottom lip was still trembling but she nodded and took off toward Rhett.

Rising, Cassidy balled her hands at her side.

She blamed herself. She had trusted Wade. Let down her guard. She had let him back into their lives. And she had let Piper get her hopes up about Wade coming to the party. Piper had gotten attached to Wade and Cassidy should have known better than to allow such a thing to happen.

Had she missed warning flags?

For the last three weeks, Wade had been the model example of dependability and hard work. He had gone out of his way to take care of her and Piper. Why couldn't he come through when it mattered most?

Was he actually sick? Even if he had a fever, he could have stopped by. Doubt gnawed at her. A normal person would have texted back their symptoms when she had told him to come anyway.

If he had been in a car accident or was stranded somewhere, he would have told her. He could have called. Instead he had given her radio silence for four days and when she had reached out, he hadn't explained himself. What had he been doing in Houston?

Ice ran through Cassidy's veins.

What if Wade was gone again?

Gone for good.

What if this whole time—

She spun away from the party and swiped at her tears. Cassidy charged away from the crowd, so no one would be able to hear the pitiful sob that ripped from her chest. Her shoulders shook as she blindly stumbled forward.

She had kissed him. Her fingers went to her lips. Kissed him a lot.

I love you. I never stopped.

Wade was a liar.

Wade was gone.

The two thoughts chased themselves around in Cassidy's head. Louder and louder. Cassidy had her hands on her thighs and her eyes pinched shut when a warm hand on her back made her jump.

Rhett's lips formed a tight line. "What's wrong?"

"Where's Piper?" Cassidy glanced around frantically.

"With Macy." Rhett gently guided Cassidy farther away from the party. Then he repeated, "What's wrong?"

Just her heart, falling to the ground with no one to catch it. Again.

Just her dreams crushed another time.

Just making a fool of herself like usual.

"Wade didn't come. I haven't talked to him in four days and now he didn't show up to this." Cassidy moved her hands wildly as she talked. "Who doesn't show up to their five-year-old's birthday party? I texted him and he was very vague. He says he's sick but I don't know."

She seized Rhett's wrist. "Rhett, what if he's gone? What if he took off on us again?"

"Let's try to get some answers before reacting." Rhett waved a hand in the air. "Shannon," he yelled. "Over here."

Shannon cut her way across the field from the staff housing area at a jog. When she was close enough she took Cassidy's hands. "Hey, it's okay. Believe me. Everything is going to be okay."

Cassidy jerked her hands from Shannon's grasp. "You know where he is. Don't you?"

Growing up as twins, Shannon and Wade had always been close. And Cassidy had noticed them spending more and more time together in the last ten days or so. She knew for a fact that Shannon had gone with him twice on his excursions to Houston, so she couldn't play dumb.

Shannon's gaze went right to Rhett. She bit her lip.

"Shannon," Rhett's voice rumbled. "If you know what's going on, you need to start talking."

"Now, don't freak out, okay?" Shannon spoke slowly, calmly, as if she was talking to a spooked horse. "I just saw him and he has a completely legitimate reason for not being here. He's so upset that he can't make it. It's killing him." She looked to Cassidy, her eyes pleading. "If he could be here, he would. You know he would. He loves you guys."

"You just... Wait... You *saw* him?" Cassidy blinked and looked back at the staff houses. "He's here. He's *here*—right here at the ranch—and he's choosing not to come?"

Shannon put her hands up in a stop motion. "Listen. It's not like that at all. He really isn't well enough right now."

"If he's really sick I want to see him. I want to help," Cassidy said.

Rhett placed a steady hand on Cassidy's shoulder. "Which house?"

"Seven," Shannon whispered. "But he doesn't want—"

Cassidy took off at a sprint across the yard with Rhett close at her heels. Shannon joined a second later. If any of the partygoers had glanced their way, they might have thought they were playing one of the designated games.

Cassidy burst through the front door to the seventh staff house with so much force the door hit the stopper and flung itself back behind her. Rhett caught the edge of it before it hit the frame. Both of them crowded into the small, enclosed entryway.

"You're back soon." Wade's voice came from the other room but it sounded strained.

Cassidy hurried into the living room and froze when her gaze landed on him. Wade was in a reclining chair and his skin was paler than snow. His hair was mushed in all directions as if he hadn't showered in a few days and a large white bandage covered the front side of his neck.

"Cassidy." His voice cracked. "You're not supposed to be here."

She fumbled to grab onto something nearby and finally ended up grasping Rhett's arm when he came up beside her.

"Are you hurt?" She found her voice. "What's going

on?" She couldn't think of an illness that required bandaging like he had.

Rhett's nostrils flared. "And I'd go with the truth this time, if I were you."

Shannon stumbled in behind Rhett and Cassidy. She eased her way to the center of the room so she could position herself between them and Wade, her hands out toward both parties. "I can tell, if that would be easier."

Wade braced his arms on the sides of his chair and he scooted forward so he was on the edge. He winced and his body shuddered as he moved. It took all of Cassidy's self-control not to rush over to him and help. Whatever had happened, he was clearly in a lot of pain.

They had just texted. Why hadn't he said how serious it was? This wasn't some passing sickness. Something was clearly wrong.

"I had surgery." He gestured toward his throat.

Cassidy let go of Rhett and stumbled forward a few steps. "When? Why?"

Wade closed his eyes and took a deep breath. "I didn't want to get in to all of this."

Rhett crossed his arms. "Well, looks like you don't have a choice."

"Cancer." Wade whispered the word.

"Cancer?" Cassidy's voice shook along with her legs. The word rammed through her. It made her chest ache. She stumbled her way to stand in front of Wade and then she dropped to her knees on the floor. Shaking all over, she didn't trust herself to stay standing. A wave of nausea rolled through her.

Cancer.
What if... What if....

She couldn't think it. She wouldn't.

In an attempt to focus, she placed a hand on Wade's knee. "I don't understand. You have cancer?"

Why hadn't he told them? That wasn't something people kept to themselves. Didn't he trust them? Trust her? Anger roiled inside of her chest. Hot and demanding justice. But fear had always been anger's favorite companion and the word *cancer* caused a lot of fear.

He started to nod but grimaced. "Thyroid cancer. But I had surgery last Friday." His fingertips dug into the armrest. "It could be all gone. I could be fine. There's no reason to worry and—"

Rhett cleared his throat. "You had cancer and you didn't tell us? What on earth were you thinking, Wade?" His voice got louder. "That's something you tell people. That's something you tell *family*. You need people around you when you're going through something like that. You deprived us of even the ability to pray for you right now."

Wade kept his eyes on Cassidy. "I figured I caused everyone enough hurt five years ago. I didn't want to do it again. They say this type has the highest survival rate, so I didn't see the point of worrying anyone if a surgery was going to take care of it."

Rhett pinched the bridge of his nose. "This is the only reason you came home." He dropped his hand to spear Wade with a glare. "You didn't come home to try to make things right, you came home because you had cancer."

Cassidy was going to be sick. "You came here to get better and leave. Didn't you?" She jerked her hand from Wade's knee and cupped it over her mouth.

He reached toward her but she leaned away from him. "Cass, please." His green eyes swam with moisture. "Please don't pull away, not over this."

Cassidy met his gaze and swallowed the burn of tears in her own throat. "Why else wouldn't you have told me?"

"You had so much on your shoulders." He winced. It clearly hurt to talk but he pressed on. "And you said that having me around was hard enough and I didn't want to complicate things more. I almost told you at the falls, but you told me you were afraid of something happening to me and—"

Cassidy rose to her feet and took an unsteady step back. "So you took it upon yourself to keep something from me. Thinking you were protecting me—from what? The truth?"

"I didn't want to hurt you."

"Well, you failed because I'm definitely hurt." She slammed her hand against her breastbone. "The only thing I need protection from is you and your endless belief that you know what's best for everyone. You don't, Wade. You're clueless."

"Cassidy, I honestly thought it was for the best. You have to believe me."

"Right, just like you thought it was a nice thing to fake your death."

His eyes flashed with hurt. "That's not fair." His voice was strained.

"Were you ever going to tell me? If we had kept going how we were, if we had gotten married—Wade, you would have married me and never told me you had cancer? That's so messed up."

"Cassidy, please." A tear slipped down his face.

"You don't love me." She shook her head. How could she have been so blind? She had to look away from him. "You don't do stuff like this to people you love. And you keep doing stuff like this."

"I do love you. I—"

"I—I can't do this." She held up a hand, blocking his tears and his face. "I can't be with you, Wade. I can't be with someone I can't trust." She started to back away. Shannon looked between them as if she were watching a tennis match.

Cassidy stilled her steps. There was one thing she needed to make sure he understood before she walked away. "For the record, this has nothing to do with you having cancer. If you had told me, I would have been there for you for the long haul. I would have held your hand the second you were out of surgery. They would have had to tear me from your side. The fact that you have cancer doesn't change how I feel about you. The fact that you lied and continue to lie does."

Wade got to his feet. "It wasn't like that." Tears freely fell down his cheeks. "Please don't do this. I need you."

"Clearly, you don't." Her voice shook as she asked, "Did you know you had cancer when you got here?"

His gaze dipped away. "It was suspected."

"So you were diagnosed while you were here at the ranch surrounded by people who care about you?"

"Yes, but—"

"If it had been me, you would have been the first person I told. You would have been the person I went to for support. But you didn't want that from me. You didn't even want me to know." Cassidy's tears spilled over again. Hot angry trails. "I can't do this, Wade. I can't be with you if this is how it's going to be." She swept out of the room before he could say anything else.

Rhett's voice boomed in her wake. Something about Wade listening to him spill his guts and apologizing for not trusting him when all along Wade had been keeping this from him.

Cassidy fled before she heard anything else.

Chapter Twelve

Wade wasn't sleeping again. Whenever he closed his eyes, he saw beautiful Cassidy swiping tears from her face. Tears *he* had caused. Her pain had been his fault.

I can't be with you.

Maybe he should leave once he was healed. Fade away in their memory as a disappointment they used to know. Leaving had never been a part of his plan, but it seemed as if Wade was still only good for one thing.

Letting down everyone he cared about.

His chest ached at the thought of not being around his family. Of leaving the people he loved again.

Leaving Piper.

He felt sick.

Even if it was for the best, he couldn't walk away from his daughter. He never would.

After the blowup, Rhett had insisted on moving Wade back into the Jarretts' ranch house so they could take better care of him and keep an eye on his healing. Then Rhett had made a point of making himself scarce.

Rhett was busy with the campers, but it was impossible not to feel as if Wade was being avoided intentionally.

By Thursday, Wade could raise his arms to shoulder height with minimal pain and walk around without the muscles around his neck protesting too much. He had removed the bandage on his neck, which had revealed a long thin line that ran across his throat. The incision was edged in red and the surrounding area was a wash of three different blues.

They had set Wade's recliner next to their mom's and she, at least, had been excited to have Wade nearby. At different points during the day, she would reach over and take his hand and hold on to him. He stayed there beside her even though his legs were restless. Sometimes she would hum some of the songs she used to sing to the Jarrett children at bedtime. Wade tried to let her presence and love comfort him.

Tried and failed.

He had texted Cassidy seventeen times, called her twice and had Shannon deliver a note to her house. Nothing had been answered and the note came back unread. She wasn't allowing Piper to come see him either.

Wade had lost her for good. Maybe both of them.

Cassidy would never want him back. Not after this.

Shannon padded down the steps in her pajamas. "I have someone on the phone who wants to talk to you."

Hope flooded Wade's veins. He reached for the phone and turned it toward him to be met with Boone's face. Wade schooled his features. He didn't want his brother to think he wasn't happy to talk to him, but it was impossible not to be disappointed. For a second, he had thought it could be Cassidy.

In the image, Boone hovered closer to the screen. "Shannon said to prepare myself for your Frankenstein scar but it really doesn't look that bad. I kind of dig it. You can tell people a shark tried to take your head but you won. Do the whole you-think-this-is-bad-you-should-see-the-shark bit." Boone scrubbed his hand over his grin. "Sorry. I probably should have started with something more along the lines of 'How are you feeling?'"

"Health-wise? A lot better. I have an appointment in Houston tomorrow to find out more." Wade forced a smile. "I like the shark story though. I may use it."

Boone nodded. "Send me a text or email afterward. We're praying for you here. Last night, even Hailey prayed for you at bedtime."

Wade cleared his throat. "It's good to talk to you. I thought you might still have been mad at me."

Boone focused on something outside of the phone's camera reach. "We've, ah—we've been dealing with some hard stuff here and I'm sorry I didn't call. It wasn't you." He gazed back at the phone. His brow scrunched. "You got my email though, didn't you?"

"I did." Wade shrugged. "But this is better."

Boone smiled but it didn't reach his eyes. "It is, isn't it?"

Shannon dropped down onto Wade's armrest and pulled the phone so she was in the picture too. "Something's going on. What are you not telling us?"

Boone pressed his hand over his eyes. "In light of Wade getting in trouble for not sharing big things going on in his life, I'm going to go ahead and share something with you guys. June and I have been trying to have another baby. She's always wanted a big family and if we wait until I'm out of divinity school, too much time will pass between Hailey and a sibling."

Shannon found Wade's hand and squeezed it.

On the other end of the line, Boone let out a loud breath. "We've had two miscarriages. The last one was two weeks ago and it's been really difficult for us. It's hard not to feel let down and forgotten by God, which I know is a horrible thing to say."

"Not horrible," Shannon said. "Just honest. God values honesty."

Wade sat up straighter in his chair, the muscles along his shoulders pulling taut. He had to bite down on a hiss of pain. "Boone, I don't know what to say. Let us know if there's any way we can support you."

Shannon took the phone from Wade. "What this one means is we love the three of you so much. Thank you for telling us what's going on. Our hearts are breaking with you guys. I know how much you loved those two sweet babies you never got to hold."

"Thank you. Both of you." Boone ran his hand over his short-cropped hair. "That's why you didn't hear from us. We had turned inward while we were mourning but after I heard what happened with Wade, I knew I needed to tell everyone what we were dealing with too."

They visited with Boone for a few more minutes until Boone said he had a sermon to finish writing for one of his classes.

"We can't wait to see everyone at the wedding," Boone said.

"Counting the days." Shannon waved to Boone. "See you guys soon!"

Before Shannon headed outside for the day, she squeezed Wade's hand and told him today would be a better day.

He wished he could believe her.

It was strange to think that when he had first returned home, he had thought his only desire would be to reconcile with his family. Now he had, but it still wasn't enough. He wouldn't be okay until he and Cassidy made peace.

Whatever it ended up looking like.

Wade spent the day praying for Boone and his family, praying for their mom and for Cassidy and Piper. Around lunchtime, he found a list of camper names Rhett must have left on the kitchen table and he started working his way down the list praying for each of them too. There wasn't much else he could do around the house right now.

His mom had spent most of the morning dozing but she stirred when he set a dirty bowl in the sink and it clanked loudly.

"Sorry," he whispered.

She groped for her glasses on the side table. After she put them on, she rested her hands on her stomach and watched him. "I was hoping by now you wouldn't look so sad."

Wade padded over from the kitchen. "The bruise looks worse than it feels."

His mom batted her hand. "I'm not talking about your neck. That'll all mend quick enough. I'm talking about here." She tapped her heart. "This is what needs healing."

Wade dropped into the chair beside her and stared

up at the ceiling. "Don't know, Mom. That might be unfixable."

"With God, all things are possible." She swatted his arm. "I taught you that when you were knee-high. Don't tell me you've forgotten."

Wade sighed. "I don't think I have this God stuff as figured out as I thought I did. I thought God wanted me to do this alone. It sounds stupid now when I say it out loud, but I thought He wanted me to prove my faith by soldiering through this trial mostly with only His support. But I did that and it made a mess out of everything."

She lowered her glasses to the tip of her nose so she could gaze at him over the top of them. "Let me see if I got this right. The God of the Bible tells us we only need the faith of a mustard seed and we can accomplish much, but for some reason you believed that same God told you to face a great trial on your own strength?"

"Not on my strength, on God's."

"Oh, Wade." She chuckled in an it's-cute-how-wrong-you-are sort of way. "You weren't trusting God at all."

"Yes, I was. I prayed about it every day. I read my Bible. I… Why are you still laughing?"

"Answer me this." She held up a finger. "The night Jesus was arrested, did He go to the garden to pray alone or did He bring his friends?"

"He didn't bring all the disciples," Wade said. "I know that much."

She pursed her lips and nodded thoughtfully. "So when He faced a trial, He didn't feel the need to go and tell everyone. That's important too. I don't think we need to share everything we face with everyone we meet. But He did tell his closest friends, right?"

"His inner circle."

"Who did you tell?"

Wade rested his elbows on his knees and leaned forward. "Shannon."

"She alone makes up your inner circle?" His mom touched his shoulder. "Is she the only person in your life you trust to support you? If so, we need to work on that."

"I would say you're all in my inner circle." He held his hands palms up, studying them as he talked because that seemed easier than meeting his mom's probing gaze. "My family and Cassidy. Especially Cassidy."

"But you didn't trust her in your hardest hour?"

Wade sat up and swiveled toward his mom. "I wanted to protect her. She told me how hurt she was last time…"

"Last time you lied to her?" She bobbed her head. "I don't blame her. Not one bit. And here you are, lying to her again. I can understand why she wouldn't want to deal with the possibility of that happening another time."

"No, I meant…" His words trailed off. It was about the lies, wasn't it? Not something happening to him. She had said she was worried about him getting in a car accident and things like that, but the heart of it was that she was afraid if she opened up to him, he would hurt her again. And he only hurt her when he had lied and kept important things from her.

Wade felt like the world's biggest idiot.

"Mom? I think I pushed her too far this time. She'll never trust me again." He dropped his head into his hands. "She has zero reason to."

He had disappointed the two people he had promised he never would—Cassidy and Piper. By his own hand, Wade had lost everything he cared about all over again. It was as if he was frantically paddling in the middle of an ocean storm once more, but this time no one had tossed a rope out to save him.

He was alone in the water.

All out of second chances.

"Mom, stop. Sit down. I'm going dizzy watching you." Piper grabbed the television remote and hit the Off button. Never a fan of quick movements, Cloudstorm pounced off the back of the couch and scurried toward Piper's bedroom.

Cassidy stopped in her tracks. She had been pacing again, hadn't she?

Piper tucked the remote in its spot on the coffee table. "Are we still not talking to Dad?" She crossed her little arms over her chest. "I want to talk to Dad."

"He's still healing, sweetheart." Cassidy knew that was a true statement, but she also knew that wasn't the reason why Piper hadn't been able to visit Wade. Cassidy's own pride and wounded heart made her want to keep Piper closer. She hadn't spoken to Wade since their fight. For all she knew, he was planning to pack up and head out once his throat healed.

"Shannon says he's fine to see. Shannon says you just don't want to see him. She told me that sometimes grown-ups fight. But know what? It's not fair that I don't get to see him just because you guys are mad." Piper's voice hitched on a tiny sob. "When Sheep bites Romeo, we don't stop loving Sheep. Isn't it like that?"

Wade had hurt their daughter by not showing up to her party, but Cassidy was hurting her now by keeping them apart.

Cassidy's heart twisted at the sight of her daughter's sadness. She scooped Piper into her arms. "I'm afraid it's a lot more complicated than that."

Piper dragged the back of her hand under her nose. "Sheep's teeth are pretty sharp, Mom. *And* he only bites Romeo when Romeo doesn't leave him alone. I think it's the same. Why can't I go see him?"

Cassidy wasn't sure if she was Sheep or Romeo in Piper's scenario and she wasn't about to ask. Piper missed Wade and wanted to see him, but was it wise to open their daughter up to abandonment?

Cassidy didn't know. But she had always tried to be honest with Piper, in ways she could comprehend. "Remember when your dad told you he decided to stay away and let us think he was gone for good?" Piper nodded. "I'm worried your dad might go again. We might get close and then lose him and that would hurt our hearts, so I'm trying to figure out the best way to protect your heart. Does that make sense?"

"Well, I think we lose Dad if we don't talk to him. I would be so sad if you didn't talk to me." Piper touched the ends of Cassidy's hair. "He'll go away if we don't tell him we love him. That's what I think."

A knot formed in Cassidy's chest right under her ribs. She was afraid any attempt to untie it would break her apart. Now that she knew what she was losing, would it always hurt this way?

A knock on the door saved Cassidy from having to

answer Piper. She set her down, sending her in search of Cloudstorm.

The morning from a week ago flashed through Cassidy's mind. Wade had been the one on the other side of the door, ready to take her on a date to hike at Gorman Falls. She had been so excited to spend the day with him, to see his face. At the time, she had believed they were on their way to becoming a forever family.

How had the world turned so topsy-turvy in such a small space of time?

Cassidy wiped her hands off on her jeans before reaching for the door handle. The door swung open to reveal Macy.

Her friend gave a small wave. "Mind if I come in?"

Macy squeezed Cassidy's arm as she walked past her. Rhett's fiancée had all but grown up at Red Dog Ranch. After Macy's mother had died when she was a teen, the Jarretts had moved her onto their property and treated her like family. Rhett and Macy had been best friends—completely meant to be—but they had suffered through years of stubborn miscommunication before realizing they loved each other. For a while, Cassidy and Macy had been really close, but ever since becoming engaged, Macy had been understandably preoccupied. Even though she hadn't realized it until now, Cassidy was hit with how much she had missed their friendship and how much she would have valued Macy's opinion on everything that had happened with Wade the last few weeks.

She should have sought Macy out days ago.

"I'm here because of Wade and you're going to hear me out." Macy had never been one to mince words.

She crossed her arms and lifted her chin, ready for a challenge.

"What's there to say?" Cassidy flung herself onto the couch. "I'm sure Rhett's filled you in on the details."

"Yeah, Wade was stupid. His reasons were flawed. But—and don't be mad at me for this—I really think his heart was in the right place." She held up a finger. "Remember, you're going to hear me out.

"He thought he was protecting you," Macy said. "And he was wrong. So wrong. Like socks while wearing flip-flops wrong. But think of his childhood, Cassidy. Every time he was honest with his parents or his brothers, they were disappointed with him. When we were teens, he asked them for help with his drinking problem so many times, and know what they would tell him? *Do better, Wade. Just stop, it's not that hard. Pray about it. You should be strong enough.* I think after a while when you reach out so many times and people are disappointed in you, you start learning to keep things to yourself. It's not an excuse, but I do think it factors into how he makes decisions."

"Even if that makes sense…" And it did. Completely. Cassidy had been there a few of the times Wade had gone to his parents. Often she had been the one who encouraged him to do it. "…I was never like that with him. You know I wasn't."

"Exactly my point." Macy stabbed the air with a finger. "You were the *one* person who always cheered him on. Who never gave up on him. Given that, doesn't it make sense that he would go out of his way to do whatever he thought would protect you? Even if that meant sacrificing his own happiness or support? Cassidy, you've got to see that, very misguided though he may be, everything he's done, that man has done because you're his person in this life. The question you have to answer is, is love worth it? And by *it*, I mean all the hurt and fights and growing pains that come along with letting someone into your life."

"He doesn't trust me. How do I move past that?"

"It's more he doesn't trust himself, really. I think he's afraid the real Wade is too messy for you to care about. I think he's scared."

"I love him." *Every messy bit.* "It's always been Wade and it will always be Wade. But I just don't know if I can put my heart out there again."

"Know what's kind of ironic?" Sunlight crept into the room and glinted off Macy's engagement ring. "Not long ago, the tables were turned and you were the one trying to talk to me about Rhett. You told me that if you could turn back the clock, you would have done anything to stop Wade from going on that trip. You said you would give anything for you two to have a second chance."

Cassidy swallowed hard. She remembered every word of the conversation. It was when Rhett had first returned to Red Dog Ranch and Macy was trying to convince him to continue the foster programs.

"You have a second chance." Macy leaned closer. She cocked an eyebrow. "Are you going to take it…or let it pass you by?"

Cassidy fisted her hands in her hair. "I don't know what to do."

"Close your eyes and picture what your life would

look like if Wade disappeared today and you never got to see him again."

Cassidy imagined herself heartbroken and not just her but Piper too. Wade had swept into Red Dog Ranch and made their family whole. He had been devoted to their daughter and made a point of spending time with both of them. He had offered Cassidy guidance that had set her relationship with God back on the right track. Wade had spent every bit of his free time building cabins, serving in the kitchen, holding his mom's hand and altogether doing good things.

Wade was not the mistake he had made—no matter how big it was.

Wade was a human—fallible and in need of forgiveness. In need of love.

Just like her.

She loved him and never wanted to be apart from him again.

Macy was clearly suppressing a smile. "I'll watch Piper if you want to leave."

Cassidy snatched her phone and was off the couch in a heartbeat. "I have to go to him." Cassidy slipped on her shoes.

"Hold up. He's not at the big house." Macy grabbed keys off the table and tossed them to Cassidy. "I saw Shannon and him leaving for Houston on my walk over here. Today's his appointment."

Cassidy slumped against the front door. The keys clattered against the metal behind her. "I'm too late?" She could talk to Wade when he got home, but she would have preferred to be at the appointment with him.

"I know for a fact that they had plans to make stops

at the gas station and the grocery store. You know how the twins are about their road trip snacks." Macy shook her head good-naturedly. "You can beat them if you get on the road now." Macy jerked her chin toward the phone clutched in Cassidy's hand. "I already texted you the address and suite number."

"I owe you."

"Less talk, more leaving." She flicked her hand dismissively. "Go get your man."

Piper bounded into the room and threw a kiss in Cassidy's direction. "I was listening and Macy is so smart and go get Daddy!"

Cassidy blew a kiss back and then ran out to her car.

Wade's gaze tripped over the building's many windows. A bird called out a happy tune from one of the nearby trees. Someone should tell the creature it lived outside a place where people often got bad news. Maybe tone down the lively tweeting.

Wade touched his neck. He had picked up the habit of constantly running his fingers over the skin there to check the healing and feel for abnormalities. Whatever had been growing there before the surgery should be gone, but he was certain he would be feeling around on his neck for the next sixty years. If God gave him sixty more.

Wade took a long deep breath and let it out through his mouth.

How often would Wade have to come here to be checked and rechecked? Would he need further treatment? What if the cancer had moved or grown?

Shannon cupped the small of his back, guiding him

toward the front doors. "It's gross out here." She tugged him through the doors of the cancer center and sighed when a wave of air-conditioning hit them.

Shannon strode to the front desk to check them in. Wade shoved his hands into his pockets and looked around the waiting area like he always did. He had a thing against sitting in chairs in doctor's office waiting rooms.

His heart lurched into his throat when he spotted her. Cassidy.

She had on jeans that fit in a way that Wade couldn't help but appreciate, her boots and a faded tank top. Her hair was down around her shoulders. It had only been two and a half days since he had seen her and if felt far too long.

Wade's mouth went dry.

The second their eyes met, she rose and crossed the room to where he was standing. He was glad she did because he wasn't sure his legs could work right now.

She was here. In Houston.

"What are you…" he started. She smiled softly at him. Almost reassuring him she was really there and not something he was imagining. She was so close and yet so far out of his reach. It hurt to see her and not know if she could ever care for him again. What if she wanted to cut ties for good and she hadn't wanted to do it at Red Dog Ranch where she lived? What if this was goodbye?

He finally breathed. "You're here."

Her smile widened. "I'm here."

She wouldn't smile if she was here to yell at him or tell him to get lost, would she? Hope whipped through his heart like a wild gust of ocean air.

He licked his lips. "I had no right to make those choices for you. Not when I left five years ago and not when I kept this from you." He motioned toward his neck. "You deserved my trust and honesty and I withheld both from you and I'm so sorry, Cass."

"Wade."

He had to keep going or else he would either lose his nerve or they would get interrupted. He loved his sister but she had the worst timing.

"Is there any chance for us?" Wade searched her eyes. "Any way you could ever forgive me?"

"Of course I forgive you."

"I'll never keep anything from you again."

Cassidy inched closer until she was in his personal space—not that he minded. "I have a question for you, Wade Jarrett."

"Anything."

"Are you planning to leave if you get a clean bill of health?"

His heart had already jumped to them being together. Her question brought his thoughts to a sudden halt. Cassidy had always been kindhearted. It would be like her to want to make peace with someone before parting ways. Had he read the situation entirely wrong?

Was she saying goodbye?

Wade studied the tips of his shoes while he gathered his courage. He had no right to expect Cassidy to want him back—to want to forge a life with someone who had repeatedly failed her. She deserved better and maybe if he were a better man, he would send her on her way without letting her see that he was breaking.

But he didn't want to let her go.

"Would that make you happy? Because, honest, Cass, I want to be part of your and Piper's lives, but I know I messed up and I'll do whatever makes you happy." Even if it was to get lost.

To never see her again.

"Can I get that in writing?" She ducked a little to catch his eyes. "The part about you doing whatever I want. Because I think it would be handy to have that in writing in the future."

"The future?" His voice was barely a whisper.

She grabbed his shirt near the bottom of his rib cage and walked him toward her until they were sharing air. "To answer you, no, it would not make me happy if you left. It would break my heart. What would make me happy is you giving me one of those kisses you specialize in."

Wade knew he had a huge goofy grin on his face and he didn't care. He couldn't help it. Cassidy was here and she still wanted him.

"And what type would that be?" he asked.

Cassidy's fingers trailed up his back. "The kind that'll make everyone at the nurses' station blush."

So he did.

In Cassidy's arms, he was home and safe and his failures faded away because she loved him and still wanted him and he would be the man she needed.

A nurse called his name. Once. Twice. Cassidy must have heard her before he did because she parted from him first. Her skin was flushed and it took everything in Wade not to go in for another kiss.

Cassidy held out her hand. "Can I come in with you?"

"Always." He took hold of her hand and they followed Shannon and the nurse down the hall. Shannon turned at one point and gave them a thumbs-up. Wade chuckled softly.

Once they were tucked in a small office, it didn't take long for the surgeon to appear. With Cassidy holding Wade's hand, it was hard to concentrate completely on what the doctor was saying but Wade knew how important today was, so he forced himself to focus.

The surgeon scanned his tablet as he explained the results of the pathology tests. "We removed a 2.4 centimeter carcinoma from your thyroid. No surprise there, seeing as that was the reason for the surgery." He dragged his finger over the tablet's screen. "Of the thirty-two lymph nodes we removed, six of them did test positive for cancer."

His surgeon had explained at length that it was normal for the type of cancer he had to move into the lymph nodes, so the news didn't shock Wade.

Shannon cleared her throat. "I'm sorry, but is that high?"

The surgeon shook his head. "Only trace amounts were found. By all accounts, we're considering Wade extremely low risk. Over the next year, you will need further testing and follow-ups—this type of cancer does have an eleven percent return rate, so monitoring and keeping your appointments is an essential part of your new protocol. But everything looks positive." He examined Wade's neck again. "And I couldn't be happier with how this is healing."

Wade jotted down information about his calcium levels, his thyroid medication and the possibility of needing a round of radioactive iodine in the future. He was glad Cassidy was there to hear everything, because he wanted her input on all the medical decisions he would have to make over the course of the next few months. Cassidy leaned in, listening to the doctor's instructions. She kept her arm tucked around Wade's waist while he took notes.

When they were ready to leave, the surgeon shook each of their hands and told them to contact the office with any questions or concerns.

Once they were outside, Cassidy took his hand again. "What are you thinking?"

Wade pulled her up short so she would turn to face him. "I'm thinking you're the most beautiful woman I've ever seen. I'm thinking you've handed me the greatest gift and I better not mess it up this time. I'm thinking I want to head home, so we can pick up Piper and all go for ice cream."

She reached out and grabbed a fist full of his shirt, drawing him close. "I meant about the doctor, Wade."

Wade pulled a face to make her laugh. "He's definitely not the most beautiful—"

She swatted his chest. "Be serious."

He wrapped his arms around her. "That man just told me my cancer is gone for now. You're here and I love you, Cassidy. You're here and I can't think beyond that."

Shannon groaned. "How about think beyond to what car you're going home in." She jangled her keys. "Because you two are sickly cute and all and I'm ecstatic for you, but it's hot and it's another three hours home and—who am I kidding, you're driving home with Cassidy." Shannon hit the button that made a truck in the lot beep. "And that's my cue." She waved and headed toward the truck.

Wade chuckled. "My sister is something else."

"Hey, Wade?" Cassidy tossed her hands over his shoulders so she could draw lazy circles in the hair at the back of his neck.

"Hmm?" Wade was too happy for words.

"I love you too." She went up on her tiptoes and claimed his lips again.

Epilogue

W ade gulped another glass of the mango-pineapple punch Cassidy had made for Rhett and Macy's wedding reception. With the barn being brand-new, they had held the wedding and reception inside. They hadn't built the stalls yet so there was plenty of room for the party. Rhett and Macy had initially said they were going to keep it to just family, but that had quickly turned into inviting many of the foster families, because everyone considered them part of the larger Red Dog Ranch family.

Wide tables at the far end of the barn groaned under the weight of sweets and other things to eat. Wade had helped Cassidy in the kitchen with prepping food for the wedding all week. Many of the older guests visited near the seating area while the younger crowd had taken over the dance floor.

With the setup for the wedding, the ceremony and now celebrating at the reception, it had been a long day. At just over two weeks after his surgery, Wade still tired fairly easily. Today had been a lot but when his gaze landed on Rhett pulling Macy onto the floor for another dance, despite weariness settling through him, Wade couldn't help but smile.

Piper skipped to his side wearing a one-shouldered white dress with a huge puffy skirt—a mini version of Macy's wedding dress. As flower girls, both Piper and Boone's daughter, Hailey, had gotten to wear them. However, Piper still had her double braids and had worn cowgirl boots with the ensemble, whereas Hailey had her blond hair piled on her head and had worn white shiny shoes. Piper had been loving having her cousin around for the weekend and had hardly left Hailey's side, so it warmed Wade's heart when she appeared next to him.

"Know what's so pretty, Daddy?" Piper grasped his hand.

He lifted her hand so she spun around once. "You."

Piper rolled her eyes. "The twinkle lights." She looked up at the patchwork of lights he and Boone had strung from the beams. "I think we should keep them up for always."

"Not sure the animals will appreciate them as much as you do."

"Oh, Romeo will. I know it."

Wade crouched beside her. "Know what I think is prettiest?"

His daughter's eyes went wide. "The cake."

"Your mommy." Wade pointed across the room to where Cassidy was busy checking on the food. Cassidy's hair was loose, tumbling down her back. She wore a blue lace dress—she had called it a lace overlay sheath dress—but Wade didn't care what it was called. All he knew was that she was the most gorgeous woman he had ever laid eyes on and he never wanted to look away.

Piper pressed her hands to either side of his face. "You should ask her to dance."

Boone cleared his throat beside them. "I'm inclined to agree with Piper."

Wade rose to his feet. He gripped his brother's shoulder. "Have I told you I'm glad you're home?"

Boone sheepishly rubbed his hand over his close-cropped hair. "A time or two."

"I hope you guys settle close when your schooling's done."

"Us too." Boone crossed his arms, making his biceps strain against his dress shirt. Wade chuckled because his older brother was such an odd mix, being a book nerd with a weightlifter's build.

"But about Cassidy." Boone jerked his chin in her direction. "I'm with Piper. Stop letting time pass you by already."

"I don't intend to." Wade fought the sudden urge to pat the ring tucked in the pocket near his heart. He clasped his brother's hand and gave him a nod. "Don't head off in the morning without saying goodbye." Then he scooped Piper into his arms and cut his way across the dance floor toward Cassidy.

When Cassidy turned and caught sight of them she immediately started cutting through the crowd until she was right in front of them. She touched Wade's arm. "You're not supposed to be lifting anything heavy."

Piper pursed her lips. "I'm not *very* big."

Wade grinned at both of them. "Doctor said I could lift after two weeks. It was two weeks yesterday."

"Still." Cassidy's brow creased in concern.

"I just want one dance with my ladies." Wade took her hand in his free one and led her toward the other dancing couples. "I'll take it easy after that, I promise."

Cassidy drew closer and looped her arm under Piper so they were supporting her weight together. Piper tossed an arm around each of their necks. Most people wouldn't have considered what they were doing dancing—more just a family hugging on the dance floor—but Wade didn't care, as long as they were all together.

"Know what? I wish it was always like this." Piper sighed. "The three of us. How come Daddy has to go to the big house every night?"

Cassidy bit her lip. Her gaze crashed with Wade's. "I wish he never had to leave us either," she whispered.

"In that case…" A breath rattled out of Wade. If there was ever an opening, that was it. He set Piper down so he could take both of Cassidy's hands in his. "Cassidy Robin Danvers, you are the only woman I've ever loved and the only woman I ever want to love. You saw the best in me when I was at my worst. You are the kindest, bravest, strongest, most talented woman I have ever met and I—"

Cassidy put her hand over his mouth. "Yes." A tear slipped down her face, then another. "Yes, Wade."

He gingerly tugged her hand away. "I didn't get to ask yet."

She laughed, grabbed the lapels of his suit coat and tugged him in for a kiss. His arms went around her and they deepened the kiss. When they broke apart, Wade realized everyone in the room was cheering. They had stopped dancing and formed a circle around his family.

With shaky fingers, he fished the ring from his pocket and slipped it onto Cassidy's waiting hand.

The crowd cheered even louder.

"Marry me?"

She took his head in her hands. "I already said yes." She touched her forehead to his. "What about the adventures you always dreamed about? Won't you miss all that tucked away at the ranch with us? You won't get bored?"

"You and Piper are the greatest adventure of my life." He kissed her gently. "You two are my everything. I love you so much, Cass."

Piper's little arms circled their legs. "I'm so happy!" she shouted up at them.

They broke apart laughing as they lifted her between them again in a group hug. And in that moment, Wade knew he had everything he would ever need in his arms.

* * * * *

If you enjoyed Wade's story,
be sure to read the first book in
Jessica Keller's Red Dog Ranch series,
The Rancher's Legacy, *available now.*

And watch for more Red Dog Ranch books
coming in 2020,
wherever Love Inspired books
and ebooks are sold!

Dear Reader,

Since the first time I envisioned this series, Wade has held a special place in my heart. He had tried to do what he thought was right and it ended up costing him and everyone around him so much. He makes me want to walk around hugging everyone in my life. Maybe I should!

Wade also said my favorite line in the book: *Trying to outrun the hard times ends up costing us more than submission ever will.*

I know I've been guilty of trying to outrun the hard times. The last year or two of my personal life has felt like one blow after another and sometimes you just want to say "Enough already." But during the hard times is when God shapes us. We need the hard times in order to grow. And like Wade learned, it's also when we need our friends the most.

I hope you enjoyed reading Wade and Cassidy's story as much as I loved writing it. If you liked this visit to Red Dog Ranch, make sure to pick up the other books in the series—there's one for each of the siblings.

Thanks for reading!
Jess

Get 4 FREE REWARDS!

We'll send you 2 FREE Books plus 2 FREE Mystery Gifts.

Love Inspired® books feature contemporary inspirational romances with Christian characters facing the challenges of life and love.

FREE Value Over **$20**

YES! Please send me 2 FREE Love Inspired® Romance novels and my 2 FREE mystery gifts (gifts are worth about $10 retail). After receiving them, if I don't wish to receive any more books, I can return the shipping statement marked "cancel." If I don't cancel, I will receive 6 brand-new novels every month and be billed just $5.24 for the regular-print edition or $5.99 each for the larger-print edition in the U.S., or $5.74 for the regular-print edition or $6.24 for the larger-print edition in Canada. That's a savings of at least 13% off the cover price. It's quite a bargain! Shipping and handling is just 50¢ per book in the U.S. and $1.25 per book in Canada.* I understand that accepting the 2 free books and gifts places me under no obligation to buy anything. I can always return a shipment and cancel at any time. The free books and gifts are mine to keep no matter what I decide.

Choose one: ☐ **Love Inspired® Romance Regular-Print** (105/305 IDN GNWC) ☐ **Love Inspired® Romance Larger-Print** (122/322 IDN GNWC)

Name (please print)

Address   Apt. #

City   State/Province   Zip/Postal Code

Mail to the **Reader Service:**
IN U.S.A.: P.O. Box 1341, Buffalo, NY 14240-8531
IN CANADA: P.O. Box 603, Fort Erie, Ontario L2A 5X3

Want to try 2 free books from another series? Call 1-800-873-8635 or visit www.ReaderService.com.

*Terms and prices subject to change without notice. Prices do not include sales taxes, which will be charged (if applicable) based on your state or country of residence. Canadian residents will be charged applicable taxes. Offer not valid in Quebec. This offer is limited to one order per household. Books received may not be as shown. Not valid for current subscribers to Love Inspired Romance books. All orders subject to approval. Credit or debit balances in a customer's account(s) may be offset by any other outstanding balance owed by or to the customer. Please allow 4 to 6 weeks for delivery. Offer available while quantities last.

Your Privacy—The Reader Service is committed to protecting your privacy. Our Privacy Policy is available online at www.ReaderService.com or upon request from the Reader Service. We make a portion of our mailing list available to reputable third parties that offer products we believe may interest you. If you prefer that we not exchange your name with third parties, or if you wish to clarify or modify your communication preferences, please visit us at www.ReaderService.com/consumerschoice or write to us at Reader Service Preference Service, P.O. Box 9062, Buffalo, NY 14240-9062. Include your complete name and address.

LI20

Surprise fatherhood, Southern charm and a heartwarming family Christmas—read on for a sneak peek at Low Country Christmas, *the conclusion to Lee Tobin McClain's Safe Haven series!*

Cash remembered coming out to Ma Dixie's place at Christmas time growing up. The contrast with his own foster family's home had been extreme. There, six themed Christmas trees were spread throughout the house, decorated perfectly by the commercial operation that brought them out each year and took them away after the holidays. That same company had wrapped garlands around the staircase and strung lights outside the house.

It had all been grand. He remembered being shocked and impressed his first year with the family, because it had been so different from the humble holidays back in Alabama. But he hadn't been allowed to invite his brothers over; too much noise and mess, his foster mother had always said. If he wanted to see them, he had to find a ride out to Ma Dixie's, which he had done frequently.

Here, Christmas really felt like Christmas.

He opened another box of ornaments, pulled out an angel made of hard plastic and handed it to Holly to place on the tree.

"Is this your tree topper, Ma?" Holly asked, holding it up.

"Yes, it is. I usually have Pudge put it up, but…could you do it, Cash, honey?"

He did, easily reaching the top of the small tree. "Is Pudge okay?" he asked Ma. "Is that why the place isn't decorated yet? He's too sick to help?"

Ma arranged the last figures in the Nativity scene and sank down onto the couch. "That's part of it. Mostly, it's me feeling blue. I'm not used to Christmas with no kids around."

Holly tilted her head to one side. "Did you have a lot of kids?"

"Dozens," Ma said with a wide smile. "That's the beauty of being a foster parent."

"Oh," Holly said as she sank down onto an ottoman beside Ma. "Do you…not foster anymore?"

Ma sighed. "I really can't with Pudge having all these doctor appointments. I guess maybe we're getting too old for it." She looked wistfully at the tree. "I just, you know, always enjoyed having the little ones around."

Holly looked thoughtful. "Is that why you wanted to take care of Penny? Not to help me out, but to have a little one around?"

"That's part of it," Ma said, "but don't you worry about it. I understand being picky where your child is concerned."

"It's not pickiness," Holly said. "If I were being picky, who better than an experienced foster parent like you?" She reached out and rubbed Ma's arm back and forth, two or three times, an affectionate gesture that made Ma smile.

Cash came over and sat at Holly's side, leaning against the ottoman. His heart, like that of the Grinch in the movie playing muted on the television, seemed to be expanding.

He'd taken plenty of women to high-end Christmas parties and fancy restaurants. But sitting here in Ma Dixie's house, talking with her about holidays and kids and family problems, decorating the tree with her, felt different. Like coming home.

Like coming home, with Holly beside him.

He put that feeling together with the questions his brother and Pudge had been asking. He was getting the horrifying notion that he might be falling in love with Holly. But he wasn't the falling-in-love type, or the settling-down type. And Holly wasn't the type for a short, superficial fling.

So what exactly was he going to do with all these feelings?

Don't miss Lee Tobin McClain's
Low Country Christmas,
available October 2019 from HQN Books!

Looking for inspiration in tales
of hope, faith and heartfelt romance?

Check out **Love Inspired®** and
Love Inspired® Suspense books!

New books available every month!

Love Inspired®

LIGENRE2018R2